PRAISE FOR CHAD ZUNKER

"A gritty, compelling, and altogether engrossing novel that reads as if ripped from the headlines. I couldn't turn the pages fast enough. Chad Zunker is the real deal."

—Christopher Reich, *New York Times* bestselling author of *Numbered Account* and *Rules of Deception*

"*Good Will Hunting* meets *The Bourne Identity*."

—Fred Burton, *New York Times* bestselling author of *Under Fire*

AN

EQUAL

JUSTICE

OTHER TITLES BY CHAD ZUNKER

The Tracker
Shadow Shepherd
Hunt the Lion

AN
EQUAL
JUSTICE

CHAD ZUNKER

THOMAS & MERCER

Text copyright © 2019 by Chad Zunker
All rights reserved.

Published by Thomas & Mercer, Seattle

www.apub.com

Amazon, the Amazon logo, and Thomas & Mercer are trademarks of Amazon.com, Inc., or its affiliates.

ISBN-13: 9781542043083
ISBN-10: 1542043085

Cover design by Rex Bonomelli

Printed in the United States of America

To Alan Graham,
who walked me into "the camp" thirteen years ago
and opened my eyes to another world,
and to the staff of Mobile Loaves & Fishes,
who are changing lives every day
and being changed in the process.

ONE

The streets are a difficult place to live and a brutal place to die.

No one understood this more than Benjamin "Benny" Dugan. At sixty-two, he'd been living on the streets for more than fourteen years. It had been booze and drugs and the loss of family connection that had initially pushed him in that direction. A quick and destructive spiral down a path of addiction and depression. Dozens of arguments that eventually led to complete separation from the only family he still had left. A gradual drift across a vast country before he finally settled on the streets of Austin.

However, it was in this city that he'd been unexpectedly embraced by the boys in the Camp, a secret community of other homeless men like him where he'd found refuge and then restoration. The boys had helped him kick the drug thing six years ago, had gotten him squared away with Jesus, and had given him a renewed sense of purpose.

The streets had become home. Benny was at peace with that.

But not tonight. A beloved brother from the Camp had gone AWOL on them. Benny was out late searching for him. Unfortunately, he had to do this exercise every few months when one of the new guys suddenly went missing for a day or two. It was part of the recovery process. Very few got through the program without facing setbacks.

This time it was Larue, his young black friend who'd shown so much progress during the past year. As he searched for Larue, Benny prayed it was simply miscommunication and not something more serious—like Larue's demons again taking root and ruthlessly pulling the kid back into the darkness.

Larue's drug was heroin. The kid hadn't had a choice—it had started at birth with his heroin-addicted mother. She'd been killed by a pimp when Larue was a kid, and he'd bounced through foster care before jumping the system. Heroin was the worst and most addictive drug on the streets. It was so lethal that breaking the chains of bondage took more than counseling and therapy—it took a supernatural act of God. Which was why the boys had been regularly praying over Larue ever since he'd joined them a year ago.

The prayers had seemed to be working. Which made tonight all the more concerning. Larue had been scheduled for kitchen duty, but he'd never shown up. No one had seen or heard from him all day. The kid had proved to be responsible, so they all feared the worst. Every member of the Camp was out on the streets of Austin tonight, searching for him.

Benny had already checked two of Larue's old hangouts. The kid used to sleep over by the basketball courts near UT's campus, where he'd try to hustle his way into a few bucks by playing pickup basketball games with college students. Larue wasn't by the courts. Benny also tried the sidewalks around the public library, since Larue had recently become obsessed with researching all the great black musicians. But he had no luck there, either.

As it neared midnight, Benny tried a third possibility. There was a place on Sixth Street called Pete's Dueling Piano Bar—a sing-along joint with a stage that held two baby grands, where two of the city's best ivory ticklers would try to outplay each other. Larue was a talented pianist. He could play like nothing Benny had ever heard before—without ever having taken a formal lesson in his life. Larue had a special ear for music. Benny and the boys had pitched in to buy him an electric keyboard from a pawnshop. The kid was magic with it. The boys could listen to him play for hours around the campfire. Benny had started calling him the Mozart of the Streets, which everyone thought was funny—mainly because Larue had never even heard of the great composer. Larue had mentioned to Benny in private that he wanted to try out for Pete's stage one day. Larue said he'd been listening to the other players while hanging in the alley behind the bar. The kid felt that if he practiced enough, he might be able to get a gig there and finally make some real money.

Turning into the alley behind the bar strip, Benny walked around the usual dumpsters and debris. He could hear a variety of different music pouring out of the nearby bars. Pete's back door was two bars ahead of him. Benny turned around when he thought he heard someone walking behind him. He searched, but no one was there. He kept moving forward, looking for any signs of Larue. He said another desperate prayer. *Come on, kid.*

A second noise from behind startled him, sounding like the bumping of a cardboard box. Benny spun around again. He saw no one approaching. Just shadows. He wondered if, in his old age, he was starting to lose his sharp eyes. They had served him well, first in the navy, and even more so out on these cruel streets.

Maybe he was just imagining things. He'd been understandably jumpier than usual the past couple of days. Exhaling, Benny pressed forward. Pete's back door was just ahead of him. Then he heard a clear male voice call out from directly behind him.

"Benjamin Dugan?"

Benny twisted around, peering into the darkness. He spotted the outline of a man walking up to him. The man wore a black leather jacket, his hands in the pockets.

"You Benjamin Dugan?" the guy asked again, stopping ten feet away.

Benny nodded but immediately regretted it. Benjamin? No one had called him by his full name in over a decade. The name actually sounded foreign to him, like some other guy. He was just Benny, not Benjamin. As the guy stepped closer, Benny suddenly recognized the short white hair and gasped. *They'd found him.* A shiver shot up his back. His chest tightened and threatened to put him immediately on the pavement. He couldn't believe it. *They'd found him.* He'd been so careful. The plan had seemed perfect. But he'd clearly underestimated their reach.

"*Jesus,*" Benny said out loud. It was a true call for help, not just an expression of shock. Staring into the man's hard eyes, Benny knew he was about to pay the ultimate price. He was too damn old to run. And he wasn't close enough to even give the man a fight.

It was over. He'd gambled and lost.

Standing there, Benny felt a strange peace wash over him. In that moment, he didn't regret his decision. He knew he'd do it all over. He'd risk his life again for the boys at the Camp and so many others who were still living and dying on the streets every day. *There is no greater love than to lay down one's life for his friends.* Benny began to whisper the words that had compelled him to go through with all this in the first place.

The white-haired man slipped his hand out of the leather jacket and pointed the long barrel of a gun right at him. Benny closed his eyes, continued to pray, and never felt a thing.

But he heard angels singing.

TWO

Six weeks earlier

David Adams arrived in Austin at dusk on the first Saturday of fall.

Downtown was bustling with its usual energy as he slowly cruised the streets. The party crowd was as thick as ever in the bars along Sixth Street. David had enjoyed the bar district immensely the previous summer during his so-called internship. Lots of parties, live music, good food and drink, pretty coeds, and late nights. David knew those days were mostly behind him.

Hunter & Kellerman's palatial law offices were on the twenty-sixth and twenty-seventh floors of the pristine Frost Bank Tower in the heart of downtown, just six blocks south of the Texas Capitol building. Parking his truck at the curb along Congress Avenue, David sat there and listened as the worn-out old engine let out a deep sigh. Before leaving Palo Alto, David had asked a local mechanic to check out his truck and let him know if he thought it would even make it all the way to Texas. The old guy had actually laughed and told David he'd better say an extra prayer. With a satisfied smile, David thought about calling him up and saying, "How you like me now?"

Getting out of the truck, David felt physically exhausted from the two-day drive but emotionally energized. He was *finally* here. Was he smiling like an idiot? Because he felt like it. The offer from Hunter & Kellerman had been 20 percent more than his other two offers, which came from big firms in San Francisco and New York. Plus a $20,000 signing bonus. The bonus check was more money than his mother had earned most *years* while raising him and his sister in Wink, Texas, a small town of a thousand just west of Odessa—the middle of nowhere. A check worth even more than the dump of an RV trailer where they'd lived nearly his whole childhood—minus the four months they'd secretly slept in the van in the parking lot behind the old Baptist church because his mom had missed too many trailer payments.

Of course, every firm wanted him. *US News & World Report* had just ranked Stanford number two on their list of top law schools. David was top ten in his class and had been within striking distance of top five. Hell, he'd have been drawing his sights on number one if not for the countless hours he'd had to put in each week behind the bar at the Dutch Goose. David had excelled in mock court, even leading his trial team to victory at the National Mock Trial Competition last year. He was bright, hardworking, and hungrier than most. The partners at H&K knew this about him—they'd done their research. They were probably already hedging their bets that he'd break all rookie billing records. With the bar exam already under his belt, David was eager to roll up his sleeves, get started, and prove them right.

Staring up at the tall steel-and-glass office building, he smiled wide again. The building sparkled with power and affluence. He left his duffel bags and boxes in the back of the truck bed, figuring someone would have to be really desperate to steal his crap. He practically danced into the spacious lobby of the Frost Bank Tower, found the elevators, and punched the button for the twenty-sixth floor. Staring at himself in the reflection of the shiny elevator door, David licked his fingers and tried to smooth out his hair. He'd changed into a clean pair of pressed black slacks and a crisp long-sleeve blue dress shirt in a gas station restroom right outside of town.

When the elevator doors opened, David took a deep breath, exhaled, and then confidently stepped into the grand lobby of the richest law firm in town. The wealth showed everywhere—from the assortment of leather chairs, plush sofas, expensive lamps, and sprawling rugs to the oil paintings covering the walls. The best of *everything*. Although it was already seven on a Saturday evening, a friendly receptionist was still planted behind the front counter. She greeted David by name and told him that Thomas Gray would be right out to see him.

Two minutes later, Thomas stepped out from around the corner. A slender man in his midthirties with short blond hair and an easy gait, Thomas wore gray slacks and a white button-down with the sleeves rolled up to the elbows. David had been paired with the attorney last summer on several easy projects. An eighth-year associate out of Columbia Law, Thomas was a true family man with a wife he adored and two young daughters. There were pictures of his two girls all over his office. David had found Thomas to be more pleasant than most of the other cutthroat hard-asses he'd met during his time with the firm the previous year. David was grateful that the man had been assigned to him as his first-year mentor.

Thomas smiled. "David, welcome."

They enthusiastically shook hands. "Good to be here."

"How was the drive?"

"Long but good. I'm ready to get to work."

Thomas laughed. "Slow down, Mr. QB. No work until Monday."

"Okay."

David had played a year of college ball at Abilene Christian before tearing up his knee. Because of that, he'd been a ringer on the firm's flag football team last summer—something that had given him a leg up on the other interns in the popularity department.

"We need to get you over to the dinner," Thomas said. "But do you want to take a peek at your new office first?"

David shrugged, tried to be casual. "Sure, I guess."

His mentor laughed at him again. "Whatever. I know you want to sprint down the hallways to it. I remember this moment like it was yesterday. Come on!"

Thomas led him around the corner and down a long hallway lined with spacious attorney offices. H&K's associates' offices were twice as big as those at the firm in New York. Lights were out in most of them, but a few associates were still at work. Thomas opened a door near the end of the hallway, flipped on a light switch, and ushered David inside. Although he tried to act cool, David felt like a kid on Christmas morning. Goose bumps shot up his arms. A contemporary wooden desk sat in the middle, two plush leather guest chairs in front of it, with an entire wall of matching mahogany shelves off to his right. But he couldn't take his eyes off the big window. Walking over, David stared down as the sun set over Lady Bird Lake, the gorgeous stretch of the Colorado River that snakes through downtown Austin. There were a lot of folks on the running trails right now. David grinned from ear to ear. It was an impressive view and an impressive office. He kept wanting to pinch himself.

"Not bad, huh?" said Thomas, stepping up next to him.

"Not bad at all."

"You can even see the bats from here."

"Seriously?"

Thomas pointed down toward the Congress Avenue Bridge. David had watched the bats last summer. It was a cool deal. About a million Mexican bats lived under the bridge. Every night near sunset, they emerged all at once, like a black cloud, and headed out looking for food.

"Try out the chair," Thomas suggested, spinning the brown leather executive chair. He walked around the desk, plopped into a guest chair, put his feet up on the corner of the desk. "We just got these in this week. I heard Lyons tell Jaworski they each cost three grand. Imported from Italy. We basically live in these chairs day and night, so the firm wants us comfortable."

David couldn't believe he'd just dropped his butt into something worth $3,000. He'd been using a metal folding chair in his rented garage apartment the past two years.

Thomas hopped up. "The firm has a room booked for you over at the Four Seasons. You can stay there until you find yourself a place to live. You got boxes in your car?"

"A few."

"I'll send a couple of clerks down and have them brought up. Let's get to the restaurant. Things have kicked off already."

David and Thomas walked a couple of blocks over to Ruth's Chris Steak House, where the firm was hosting dinner in a private room. The entire litigation group was there, along with wives, husbands, boyfriends, and girlfriends. The dinner was an official welcome to the firm's three new hires before the partners began squeezing the billable life out of them. The addition of David and two others grew the overall litigation group to forty-five attorneys.

David spotted William Tidmore standing across the room from him. The previous summer, David had interned with Tidmore—an obnoxious jerk from Yale—and couldn't stand the guy. Tidmore came from money and made sure everyone knew it. Last summer, he'd driven a fancy BMW and never missed a chance to try to make David feel like a lower-class country bumpkin. Tall and skinny, with pale skin and perfectly combed blond hair, Tidmore was already rubbing elbows and kissing the asses of two of the partners.

H&K had also hired Claire Monroe, a short, plain-faced, red-haired gal who had graduated number one in her class at New York University Law. Claire was sharp and cunning. David was certain she was three times smarter than he was. But she did not annoy him or threaten him to the same degree as Tidmore. David knew he could outwork Claire.

David made his way over to Claire at the bar.

"Hey, Claire," he said.

"Hi, David. I was happy to hear when you accepted at H&K."

"I feel the same." He glanced over as his rival joined them. "Hey, Tidmore."

"Hey, Trailer Park," Tidmore replied, grinned.

"Boys, be nice," Claire suggested.

The Ivy League jerk had started calling him that stupid nickname last summer after finding out about David's humble upbringing. David wanted to punch him in the face each time he said it, just like tonight. But he'd have to take it out on him in other ways. The partners had strategically placed their offices right next to each other, a clear attempt at encouraging their cutthroat competition. David knew they would push each other to the limits. He looked forward to it. Between studying and bartending, he'd already learned to live off four hours of sleep. He was determined to bury that snobby punk.

A few minutes later, Marty Lyons took command of the dinner from the front of the room, and all voices silenced. Lyons had personally recruited David to Hunter & Kellerman. As head of litigation, Lyons had twice been on the cover of the *American Lawyer*. With prestige, power, and incredible wealth, he embodied everything David hoped to become one day. The job offer the partner had made over dinner several months ago was one of the great moments of David's life. It had made him feel instantly rich after a lifetime of being dirt-poor. Lyons had dark hair with a few touches of gray above the ears and wore a perfectly tailored blue suit. David knew from interning last summer that the partner owned an entire closet of expensive suits. David had counted four different Rolex watches on the man's wrist at different points. He'd spotted Lyons behind the wheel of both a $100,000 Mercedes and a shiny black Porsche 911 Turbo. He'd heard that Lyons owned a thousand-acre ranch in south Texas and a five-thousand-square-foot cabin in Vail.

Lyons said a few nice things about each of the new associates, officially welcomed them to the greatness of the firm, made a toast toward the upcoming year, then invited everyone to eat and drink to their hearts' delight. Two buffet lines opened, serving lamb chops and salmon filets, among other delicious items. David loaded up a plate and sat with Thomas and his wife, Lori, who invited David to their home for dinner on Sunday night. Lyons came by to give him another heartfelt welcome and told David how excited he was to have him as part of the family. The eating and drinking lasted several hours until everyone started making their way for the exits, some stumbling out the doors because they'd spent too much time at the bar.

David was on the sidewalk outside the restaurant when he spotted one of the other associates having a difficult time getting into his Lexus sedan at the curb. The guy slumped over, banged up against the car door, uttered some curse words. He was clearly drunk.

"You okay, bud?" David asked, walking up to him.

He looked over, eyes red. "Just splendid."

The guy was in his early thirties, with neat black hair.

"Carlson, right?" David asked.

The guy nodded. "Yep. Nick Carlson."

"I'm not sure it's a good idea for you to climb behind the wheel right now."

"I'm fine, I swear."

Just as soon as he'd said that, Nick stumbled forward again, and David caught him before he took a serious nosedive straight into the concrete.

"How about I give you a ride, Nick?"

"Sure, if you insist."

With one arm holding the man upright, David guided Nick a block over to where his truck was parked along the curb in front of their office building. He helped Nick get into the passenger seat and then pulled the seat belt around his plump body. Nick immediately slumped over against the window. Climbing in next to him, David started up the truck.

"Where to, my friend?" David asked.

"Far West," Nick mumbled, managing to give David his address.

David drove out of downtown proper, caught the MoPac Expressway north, and headed up the highway toward Far West Boulevard.

"Nice truck," Nick said, sitting up a bit. "Reminds me of my dad's. He loved that truck. God rest his soul."

"Your dad passed?"

Nick nodded. "A few years ago."

"Well, your dad had good taste."

"And class, too," Nick added. "Hell, I wish I was half the man he was."

"Come on, I'm sure he'd be proud of your success."

"Not if he knew the truth . . . ," Nick muttered, staring out the side window.

David tilted his head. Nick was a sad drunk. "I guess you're not from money?"

Nick laughed. "Hell no. My dad was a truck driver in Mississippi." He had trouble saying the *Mississippi* part, his speech was slurring so much. "I had to earn all of this the hard way, probably like you." He turned more fully to David. "Listen, man, you can't let jerks like Tidmore get to you. I heard him sticking it to you again over by the bar. Guys like Tidmore are a dime a dozen around firms like Hunter & Kellerman. Families worth so much damn money that they get hired by partners just with the hope that the firm can pick up the family as clients. Annoying as hell, but just part of it."

"Yeah, that guy really pisses me off. But I guess I've just got to get used to the ribbing."

"I wouldn't. I'd just leave."

David looked over at Nick. He sat there stone-faced and wasn't joking.

"I'm not going to let jerks like Tidmore run me off."

Nick sat very still, eyes forward. "I'm not talking about Tidmore. The firm is dark, man. So very dark. Before you know it, Lyons will take your soul. You should get out before you run into real trouble—like me."

"What kind of trouble?"

"Nothing, man. Just talking."

David finally pulled up to a small but nice redbrick house along a well-kept street of other nice little houses. He parked at the curb out front, damn near had to carry Nick to the front door, and then helped him use his key to unlock it.

"You going to be all right, bud?" David asked.

Nick looked up with bloodshot eyes. "Time will tell." He reached out, grabbed David by the arm. "I'm serious, man. You should leave. Now. Before it's too late for you, too."

"Go sleep it off, Nick. I'll see you at the office, okay?"

"Yeah, all right."

After shutting the door behind Nick, David returned to his truck. He was halfway back downtown when he looked over and realized Nick had left his wallet on the passenger seat. Sighing, David turned the truck around, drove back up to Far West, and again parked along the curb in front of Nick's house. He knocked firmly several times on the front door, but there was no response. Nick was probably already passed out on the floor somewhere, although David thought he saw shadows of movement through a side window. He knocked again. Still no answer. Spotting a mail drop box next to the front door, David placed the wallet inside and then returned to his truck. He pulled out his phone, scrolled through a personal phone number list he'd been given by the firm, and typed out a quick text to Nick to give him a heads-up about the wallet.

Before driving away, he peered toward Nick's house one more time and noticed a figure suddenly emerge from around the side, as if coming from the back. David squinted. Was that Nick? When the guy passed briefly under a security light by the garage, David realized it was not. This guy was thinner, with short white hair. Could Nick have a roommate? He hadn't mentioned anything. The guy gave a quick glance over in David's direction and then tucked back into the shadows and disappeared down the sidewalk.

THREE

Frank Hodges stood at the balcony doors inside the presidential suite at the Driskill Hotel in downtown Austin. Night was upon the city, and Frank could see Austin's famed Sixth Street below him, bustling with raucous activity. Music blared from every bar venue, and the sidewalks were busy with people. At sixty-seven, Frank was not in town to party. He was here on business. A potential new client had flown him in from Florida earlier that evening. Frank checked his wrist. The man who'd rented the expensive suite for this private meeting would be arriving at any moment. The client had insisted on meeting in person and limiting phone and email communication. This was not uncommon in Frank's line of work. All his clients had become paranoid about hackers. He couldn't really blame them. As long as they paid his expensive sit-down fee, he would gladly jump on a plane.

Frank had spent nearly forty years with the CIA, where he'd run point on covert operations in more than two dozen countries. Although he was not ready to quit the Agency, Frank had been pushed into retirement a few years earlier. It was a young man's game now, he'd been repeatedly told by his smug new supervisor—a guy twenty-five years younger who'd never even been in a hostile situation. His new boss had somehow worked his way up the ranks from behind the protection of a damn computer screen. He'd never slept in a cramped prison cell in an obscure third-world country for seventy-eight straight days while his government had tried to secretly get him out. He'd never had to kill a man to protect his own identity and complete an assignment. His supervisor hadn't been shot four different times and been left with the scars and limp to prove it. At his so-called retirement party, after a few too many drinks, Frank had seriously thought of breaking his boss's neck and stuffing him in the trunk of his car. Thankfully, he'd had two friends there who'd wisely dragged him away.

After leaving DC, Frank had bought himself a small condo along the Florida coast and tried his hand at fishing. He'd had an old Agency friend, who'd also been forced into retirement, who loved fishing for tarpon and somehow seemed content with just kicking his feet up and casting a rod every day. So Frank had thrown his own line in the water and waited. But forty years' worth of adrenaline does not fade fast, he'd quickly learned. Like an aging NFL quarterback struggling to retire, Frank got bored within months and wanted back in the game. He couldn't stand the thought of spending his final days sitting next to other lifeless old men who drank cheap beer, wore flowery silk shirts, griped about the weather, and listened to Jimmy Buffett all day. Frank's version of "Margaritaville" was sitting in an unmarked van doing surveillance on a potential perp. Or chasing a mole through a dark alley and wrangling the truth out of him.

Frank put the fishing rod away and instead put up a shingle for private security consultation. Special ops for the private sector. It was a dark and dirty world out there, and men with his unique skill set and experience had become extremely valuable. Frank could be hired only by those in the know who had serious money and real problems to solve. He wasn't interested in trailing cheating husbands for broken-hearted wives. Frank ran only legit operations. Since opening, his firm had been inundated with job opportunities. Frank had actually made more money in the last few months than he'd made during almost forty years with the Agency.

Turning away from the balcony, Frank took a look at himself in a mirror on the wall and straightened his black sport coat. Although his hair had turned gray a long time ago, he still had a full head of it. Most of his friends couldn't say the same. His build had remained lean and muscular—he ran three miles a day on the beach back in Florida. His brown eyes, though wrinkled, were every bit as sharp as they'd been when he'd joined the Agency as a young man. His Brazilian girlfriend, Maria, said she loved his eyes. She was thirty years younger. He loved absolutely everything about her.

Frank turned when the door to the hotel suite opened. A midfifties man entered wearing a suit and carrying a black briefcase. Frank shut the doors to the balcony for complete privacy. The two men shook hands, exchanged brief greetings, and then sat on opposite sides of a coffee table in the dimly lit living room. The man in the suit was all business, which was just fine with Frank.

"Thanks again for meeting me on such short notice, Mr. Hodges," the man said. "I know you have your choice of clients, as your reputation is absolutely stellar, so I appreciate your flying out here to discuss this with me in person."

"Tell me about your situation," Frank said, hands crossed in his lap.

"We're being blackmailed."

"Sorry to hear that."

"We need you to find some people for us as quickly as possible."

"How many people?"

"Six men, in particular."

"These men know each other?"

"They served together in the navy a long time ago."

The man opened his briefcase, pulled out a faded color photograph, and slid it across the coffee table to Frank. He picked it up and studied it. In the photo, seven young sailors all stood together on a dock. There was nothing distinguishable about them or their location. From the look of their uniforms, Frank guessed the group photo had been taken in the midseventies, which would make these men all around his age now.

"I count seven," Frank mentioned.

"We do not need you to find the second man from the right."

"You have any names?"

"Only for three of the men, unfortunately. We need you to find these guys and figure out if one of them might be behind the blackmail effort."

"Has an ask already been made?"

"Yes. We're prepared to pay it—for now. We'd like you to handle the exchange."

"When?"

"Tomorrow morning."

"Not a problem."

The man opened his briefcase, pulled out a manila envelope, and slid it across the table to Frank. "Everything you need to know is in there."

Frank leaned back in the leather chair. He knew better than to ask the obvious questions. He was paid a lot of money to handle matters for wealthy and powerful people without having to know their reasons behind them, unless they were relevant to his completing an assignment. Most times, the less he knew, the better he slept at night. Plus, it protected him from being in the line of fire should one of his clients end up in a courtroom or find him- or herself sitting in front of a congressional panel. Staring at the photograph, he felt this was a rather easy job. These were all old men. Finding them shouldn't be too difficult. His crew was in between operations right now, so he could have them jump on this immediately.

"You're comfortable with my financial requirements?" Frank asked.

"Yes. The money will be wired to your account tonight. We need this handled as quickly and as quietly as possible. Both time *and secrecy* are of the essence."

Frank nodded. All his clients said that.

"We'll get started right away."

FOUR

David arrived at the firm at five thirty on Monday morning.

The office was eerily quiet. No one was there yet—except for Tidmore, which really pissed David off. He couldn't believe the guy had actually beaten him to the punch on their first official day with the firm. Ignoring the light coming from his rival's office, David circled his desk and began to get himself organized.

Tidmore was standing at his doorway a second later.

"I was wondering if you were ever going to show up."

David looked up, shook his head. "You sleep under your desk?"

"No, but I'm not opposed to it to get the job done."

"It's a marathon, not a sprint."

Tidmore gave him his usual cocky smile. "You keep telling yourself that, Trailer Park, while I go submit my first hour of billable work."

"You go do that, Tidmore."

Rolling up his sleeves, David took his first billable action as a new attorney. Thomas had already dumped six thick expandable folders on his desk—discovery for one of their cases. He wanted David to take a crack at drafting a motion of summary judgment by Thursday morning. David stared at the massive pile. It would take him two days just to review it all. The client was a huge software company worth billions.

Fortunately, a company worth billions gets sued weekly. For his work, David would bill them $475 per hour—more than he had made bartending in a full week. Thomas billed $700 per hour. Partners at H&K billed up to $1,200 per hour. Was any human being really worth that? It was standard firm policy to bill clients in six-minute increments. If David even thought about a client in the shower for a few seconds, he was supposed to hit them with a sixer, which basically meant in the time it took him to shift the heavy folders around his desk, he'd already made the firm seventy-nine dollars. He was off and running!

The office came to life around eight. His administrative assistant was Margie, a portly woman with red hair. In her midforties, she'd been with the firm for over twenty years. Margie had an edge to her and took to bossing David around immediately. Thomas said she was one of H&K's best and brightest and probably knew more about the law than David ever would. He was lucky to have her, Thomas suggested. His paralegal was a sharp young Brazilian guy named Leo, who immediately began helping David get his office organized and caught him up to speed on all the litigation cases. Leo had been with the firm for six years and knew all the nuances and oddities of each associate and partner, which he gladly shared with David. He liked Leo from the beginning.

At nine, Marty Lyons called an urgent meeting for all attorneys to immediately gather in the main conference room. The whole group huddled around a long conference table, where they gossiped about why Lyons had called the meeting. Was there a big new case? Lyons finally walked into the room, looking somber, and made his way to the head of the table. The room fell silent.

"I have difficult news to share with you all and wanted to do it in person this morning. Yesterday afternoon, police informed me that Nick Carlson took his own life on Saturday night."

A chorus of gasps bounced around the room. David's was one of them.

"I won't get into the details," Lyons continued. "But this is obviously a tragic situation for all of us. Nick was a terrific attorney and was well liked around here. He will be sorely missed. I will keep you posted on funeral arrangements as they come together with his family. You'll be receiving an email from HR in a few minutes to connect you to counseling services, should any of you need help with handling a horrible situation like this one, as well as the ongoing stress that comes with our jobs here. I only wish we'd been able to get Nick the help he clearly needed before it was too late."

With that, the meeting was over, as everyone just stared at each other in disbelief.

Thomas came over to David. "Not exactly the first day I'd hoped for you."

"It's shocking."

"For all of us."

"How did he do it?"

Thomas sighed. "I heard he hung himself on Saturday night."

"But he was drunk as hell, Thomas."

"Was he? How do you know?"

"I drove Nick home that night, helped him get into his house."

"Damn. Really? You may have been the last person to see him alive. Police said his girlfriend found him yesterday morning."

David thought about the guy he'd spotted outside Nick's house.

"Did Nick have a roommate?" he asked Thomas.

"I don't think so. Why?"

"Nothing. This is just . . . hard to believe. Did you see it coming?"

Thomas shook his head. "Of course not. I mean, we're all stressed the hell out. But I never suspected anyone would take it this far. I wish I'd known. Maybe I could've helped him out somehow, lightened his workload, or just talked some sense into him. I don't know."

"Maybe it was more than just work."

"Maybe. But there was a note, and Nick blamed the stress of work."

"He left a note?"

"Yeah, he typed it out on the firm's letterhead."

David pondered the note. Could Nick have possibly pulled it together enough to type out a suicide note after David had dragged him to his front door? That seemed unlikely. Maybe he'd written it in advance and already planned to end things that night. Nick certainly hadn't seemed to be in a good emotional place.

"You going to be okay?" Thomas asked.

"Yeah, sure. I mean, I barely knew the guy."

But all David could think about was what Nick had told him in the final moments of his life. *You should leave. Now. Before it's too late for you, too.*

FIVE

Frank was situated in a dark hotel room near the airport. A bank of computers was set up on a table in the corner. He sat behind a keyboard and pulled up a surveillance video on the center screen of the money drop yesterday morning, one that he'd probably watched more than a thousand times already. The video started with a view from a balcony ledge over the back side of a crowd of people who were all sitting in wooden pews inside an old church sanctuary. It was a traditional church setting. Lots of red carpet, ornate crosses, communion tables, stained glass windows, and a robed minister standing up front behind a wooden lectern.

Frank had planted one of his guys with a hidden surveillance camera in the empty balcony. He'd had three more guys seated in the crowd. One of Frank's top field operatives, Wilson, had been in the second row on the left side of the church's lower level. The surveillance video zoomed in on the back of Wilson's head for a moment. Sitting by himself, Wilson wore a dark suit and tie and looked like he belonged. Two older folks sat on the opposite end of the row from him. The sanctuary had two sections of wooden pews, with one center aisle and two outside aisles. Frank had calculated 189 people sitting on both sides of the center aisle. Ninety-four women, eighty-one men, and fourteen children.

Seconds later, the surveillance video showed several men holding red velvet church bags walk up the aisles to the front of the sanctuary. The robed minister said a long-winded prayer, and then the men turned and began passing the offering bags.

Frank's attention was on only the left side. He watched closely as Wilson carefully dropped a thick brown envelope into an offering bag. Frank had placed a black X on the outside of the envelope, as instructed. The velvet bags were passed slowly down each row as the ushers gradually made their way toward the back of the sanctuary. Quick research on the church told Frank it was over a hundred years old—it looked like more than half the people in attendance yesterday had been there from the beginning. Frank was running names of every member listed in the church's directory through their software, seeing if any matched the names they already had from the navy photograph. It was a long shot. The church had over twelve thousand names on an archaic roster that went back more than eighty years.

Frank squinted at the computer screen. No one hurried with the bags. More than a dozen times, an old man or woman paused for several seconds while counting out change from a purse or a wallet before moving it forward. It took the congregation six minutes and thirty-seven seconds to get the bag to the back of the room. The bag on the left side was passed in front of 103 people. Seventy-one individual hands had actually reached inside up to wrist level—from what they could tell by enhancing the surveillance footage. Frank never spotted the brown envelope being lifted. Neither did any of his guys seated in the rows. However, when the bag got to the back of the room, the X envelope was gone—along with the $10,000 in crisp $100 bills that had been placed inside of it. Wilson had confirmed it with an usher afterward.

Again, Frank saw nothing new in the footage. He sighed, shook his head. Someone had somehow managed to snag it. They'd narrowed it down to thirty-nine potential candidates. Thirty-one men and eight women of various ages. They were creating sparse profiles on all thirty-nine candidates. It was a ridiculous starting place. Whoever had initiated the cash drop yesterday was no fool. This wasn't your everyday drop-a-bag-at-the-corner-and-walk-away type of deal. The complicated exchange had all the fingerprints of a professional.

Frank did know one thing for certain. This wasn't about $10,000. Someone was using today to simply test the market.

Which meant a much bigger ask was forthcoming.

SIX

David's first day at the firm was a bit of a blur between absorbing the news about Nick's suicide and trying to get himself settled into his new workload. Although most of the associates and staff walked around in a daze much of the day, there were still clients to be served. So the immaculate hallways began seriously humming again around noon. Phones were ringing incessantly, copiers and printers were spewing paper, keyboards were being pounded, coffeepots were constantly brewing, clerks and assistants were running up and down hallways, and partners were yelling at their phones, at associates, and even at each other. Margie ordered David a deli sandwich when she actually heard his stomach rumble while inside his office.

As if by planned strategy, almost every hour on the hour, a new partner or senior associate would drop by his office unannounced, say something like, "I need this by tonight, Stanford," and set a thick folder or binder on his desk. The folders and binders piled up against the window behind him. By the end of the day, David would be able to build a fort with them around his desk. He figured he might as well use them to wall off the exit, because he wouldn't be leaving the office for a *long* time. Leo practically lived in the office with him all day, laughing at times at the carousel of superiors dumping work on him.

Margie left him at six. Leo stayed until seven before saying he had to get to his son's Little League game. Dinner was catered by the firm—it was standard practice, always billed to clients. No one was expected to be gone by dinner. David ate a salad and some pasta and sucked down probably his tenth cup of coffee.

Thomas poked his head inside David's office around eight.

"Knock, knock, counselor."

David looked up, his hair disheveled, a coffee stain on his shirtsleeve.

"My draft done yet, rookie?" Thomas asked.

David frowned. "You said Thursday."

Thomas smiled. "I'm joking—relax."

David sighed, rubbed his eyes. "Hard to relax when one of your buddies is dumping something on my desk every ten minutes. I've already got enough work for the next six months."

"Welcome to Hunter and Kellerman."

"Right."

Thomas shrugged. "Fine, I'll give it to Tidmore instead."

"Hell no, I'll get it done."

Thomas laughed. "You'll get used to the pace of this place. They're all just testing you, seeing which of you rookies works best under pressure. We're all placing bets on who will crack first. You're *my* horse, David, so don't let me down. But to be honest with you, Tidmore has much better odds around the office right now."

"You're kidding me?"

"Man, you're way too easy today," Thomas said, smiling. But then he pressed his lips together. "Considering the news of the day, I probably shouldn't be joking about people cracking up in any way." He glanced at his wrist. "I've got to get home and tuck my girls into bed. In all seriousness, QB, don't let the pressure get to you. You don't have to be a superhero, trust me. Just work hard, work smart, be patient, and know when to go home for the night."

Most of the other associates and partners began peeling off around nine—that seemed to be the hour they all started letting each other off the hook. By ten, the office was basically empty. Of course, the lights stayed on in the side-by-side offices of the firm's two newest star recruits until well past midnight. The race for rookie of the year had officially begun, and neither man wanted to give ground on the very first day—even if one of their fellow associates had wigged out. David could barely keep his eyes open as he stared at the paperwork on his desk. But he didn't even consider leaving. Finally, around one thirty in the morning, he noticed the light turn off next door.

"See you in a few hours, Trailer Park," Tidmore sneered, passing by his doorway.

David waited another half hour and then finally called it a day. If he stayed any longer, Margie might find him drooling all over his desk the next morning.

On the way to the elevator, David spotted the light on in another associate's office. He wondered if someone else was really working even later than he was. As he neared the door, he noticed that the nameplate on the outside wall belonged to Nick Carlson. Someone was inside Nick's office? Peering in the doorway, David found a guy probably in his thirties wearing a black jacket and a black ball cap rummaging through paperwork on the desk. Several of the desk drawers were pulled out and sitting on top of the desk. When the guy noticed David's presence at the doorway, he looked up with narrowed eyes.

"You need something?" he asked.

"Nope. Just headed home. Was surprised to find someone else still here in the office."

"Building security," the guy clarified.

"Oh, all right."

"Have a good night, sir," the guy said. But it sounded more like *Get lost.*

Walking away, David began to ponder why the guy looked somewhat familiar. Was it from seeing him in the building lobby's security booth?

SEVEN

After a grinder of a first workweek, David decided to join a group of other H&K associates at Buffalo Billiards on Sixth Street on Friday night. Thomas had suggested it would be good for him to start building some alliances within the firm, as men who put themselves on islands tended to get taken out more easily. Big-money law could be really cutthroat. David needed more than just Thomas sitting in his corner. It was admittedly hard for David to pull himself away from his desk, as he was more determined than ever to beat Tidmore to a pulp his first month at H&K. The guy took every chance he could to rub him wrong. Although billing entries were kept private among partners, David had heard through the grapevine that he and Tidmore were currently running neck and neck.

Thankfully, Tidmore also joined them, which allowed David to relax a bit. At least he wouldn't be falling behind. A group of about eight attorneys tossed back pitchers of beer, played pool, and threw darts. A pool tournament broke out among them, with a lot of trash talking, and David found himself consistently knocking balls into pockets and wiping out the competition. He used to hang out after hours at the Dutch Goose and play pool with the other staff back in Palo Alto, so he'd gotten pretty good with the stick.

Everyone, including David, got a bit distracted when an attractive blonde in a short cocktail dress and high heels came over and began watching them all play. She looked to be in her midtwenties, like him. Tidmore made the first move, sidling up to her, flashing his perfect Yale smile, and trying to make small talk. Rolling his eyes, David grabbed another beer from the bar—he was getting a bit tipsy.

As luck would have it, the pool competition resulted in a show-down between Tidmore and David. Tidmore kept bragging about how he'd had private lessons from some famous professional player back in Boston. Just another in a long line of ridiculous perks from his affluent upbringing. One of the associates asked David where he learned to play, to which David explained he was self-taught. Tidmore took an opportunity to mock him again.

"David probably learned playing with truck drivers at some West Texas redneck joint after he was done cleaning the toilets each night."

A few guys laughed. Others told Tidmore to take it easy. David felt his blood boil—especially because the blonde was still watching everything closely. They'd made eyes at each other a couple of times, shared a quick smile, but he hadn't talked to her yet. David had a good buzz going right now, and if Tidmore pushed him too far, things might get out of hand quickly. Exhaling a deep breath, David knocked in the eight ball and beat Tidmore. David got a few congratulations, but Tidmore wouldn't let up about it.

"This never would've happened if I had my own stick with me," Tidmore stated.

"You lost, Tidmore," David said, shaking his head. "Just deal with it."

"Whatever," Tidmore snapped. "You may beat me at pool, you may somehow manage to put in more billable hours than me, but it will never change the fact that you'll always just be trailer-park trash. And nothing you do will ever change that fact. So deal with *that*."

Within seconds, David had grabbed Tidmore by the shirt collar and flung him on top of the pool table, ready to take his damn head off.

Thankfully, several of the other associates grabbed him from behind and dragged him away before he did any real damage—to Tidmore's face or to his budding legal career. One guy pushed him across the room and over to the bar, where he began to cool off and catch his breath.

A delicate hand touched his shoulder from behind. He turned and found the blonde standing there.

"Anyone sitting here?" she asked, nodding toward the empty stool next to him.

"Uh, no . . . please . . . have a seat."

She sat next to him. "That was quite the scene back there."

David shook his head. "I'm embarrassed you saw that. I should have never lost my cool that way."

"Don't be. That guy was a jerk. I wanted to punch him myself."

They shared a smile. She had perfect teeth.

"I'm David."

"Melissa," she replied.

"Can I buy you a drink?"

"Sure. I'll have what you're having."

David quickly ordered up two more beers.

"You here by yourself?" David asked.

"I am now. I was hosting a couple of clients earlier who like this sort of thing."

"What kind of clients?"

"I'm a financial adviser. What about you?"

"An attorney with Hunter and Kellerman." He intentionally mentioned the name of the firm in hopes of impressing her. It seemed to work.

"I know that firm well. How long have you been with them?"

"Just started this week. Drove in last weekend from Palo Alto."

"Stanford?"

"Correct."

"Now you're just trying to show off, David."

"Is it working?"

She grinned. "So far."

They made a bit of small talk about Palo Alto. Melissa mentioned she had done her undergrad at Vanderbilt and was currently getting her MBA from UT. It was an easy conversation. David enjoyed it even more when he spotted Tidmore staring at them from across the room.

"Have you found a place to live yet?" Melissa asked.

"Not yet. I've been staying over at the Four Seasons. But I was hoping to look around this weekend. Don't want to stay in the hotel forever."

"I know a great Realtor. How about I call her up, and we can show you a few places?"

"Really? That'd be great."

"Will Sunday work?"

"Sure."

They exchanged business cards.

"I'm really beat, David. It's been a long week for me, so I'm going to take off. No more bar fights, okay? I'd hate for you to miss our first date because you've been tossed in jail."

They shared a flirty smile.

"I'll try," he replied.

David watched her walk out. Across the way, he noticed Tidmore continuing to stare, so David gave him a wink and a grin. His rival flipped him the bird, which made David smile even wider. There was nothing better than seeing that guy's pale face flush red with anger.

EIGHT

Frank Hodges again met his client in the presidential suite at the Driskill Hotel. It was nearing midnight. The curtains were all drawn, the suite dark except for a few lamps situated around the living room. Frank slid a folder across the coffee table—a full report on everything his team had gathered in their search thus far. His client picked up the folder, began to slowly review its detailed contents. Frank had easily found two of the men from the photo: both were long dead. One seaman had died in a farming accident more than twenty years ago in Iowa. A tractor trailer had tipped over and completely crushed him. The other navy boy had died from cancer of the liver eight years ago while living in Mississippi. Frank had copies of both death certificates. A third man from the photo lived in Casper, Wyoming, where he'd owned a successful insurance business for more than thirty years and had a very public profile. Two men lived in Texas—one near Houston, the other outside of Dallas. One of them was a complete drunk who couldn't seem to hold a job. The other was a salesman for a printer company who lived a rather dull middle-class life.

"We've found all but one so far," Frank explained, pushing the conversation along. "We have addresses, contact info, photos, and we've put together detailed profiles on each of these men. Everything is in the report."

"Who's still missing?"

"A man named Benjamin Dugan. He disappeared near Memphis around fifteen years ago after his wife died from cancer. Those who knew him back then said he fell hard into drugs and alcohol and lost everything. Dugan started living on the streets until one day he was just gone. No one seems to know what happened to him. He doesn't collect any state or government funds or benefits. No license renewals on record. We have loose trails into Arkansas, Mississippi, and Oklahoma. Dugan has an adult daughter who still lives in Memphis. She says she hasn't heard from her father in years. She believes he's dead. We'll continue to hunt him down until we confirm it."

The other man nodded. "What about the money drop?"

"The two men in Texas are the most likely culprits—simply because of geographic proximity—although I suppose any of these men could've used an outside player to pull off this kind of job. As you'll read in the report, the two men in Texas both have money issues. Our boy in Wyoming does not. But you can never be certain with the motivations on this kind of thing."

"Can you confirm any of these men being in or around Austin?"

"Not yet. Mind you, my team was not yet tracking each man closely, as we had just gotten started. However, I do have a man on each of them now. So far, the ten grand in cash hasn't shown up. We're monitoring bank accounts. If it's one of these three guys, we'll eventually discover it. We just need to be patient."

"It's not necessary," said the man, stuffing the report and photos back into the folder. "We already have what we need. Final payment will hit your account tonight."

"You want us to pull out?" Frank questioned, surprised.

"Correct." The man stood. "Good day to you, Mr. Hodges."

Gathering his briefcase, the man quickly left the hotel suite.

Still sitting there, Frank pondered his unexpected dismissal. Something didn't sit right in his gut. There was still work to do if his client truly wanted to identify who was behind the extortion. Why not let him finish the job? All he needed was more time. Standing, Frank walked over to the bar and poured himself a glass of Scotch. He got paid *a lot* of money to do his job without asking unnecessary questions. That's the only way the system worked with private security. Most days, Frank considered it a beautiful marriage. But these were navy veterans. Men who'd served their country, much like he had. Was his client desperate enough for an immediate resolution that he would go to extremes to get it?

NINE

Melissa lived in a picturesque three-bedroom yellow house with a white fence out front in an affluent neighborhood near downtown. The lawn was meticulously landscaped, with colorful flowers in all the beds, the sidewalks all properly edged. The property looked pristine. A shiny burgundy Land Rover sat parked underneath a carport. David spotted a tiny white poodle yapping away from a window beside the white front door. David knocked twice. Melissa opened the door looking gorgeous in a short white dress with heels.

"You ready to find your own place?" she asked, smiling.

"I guess so. Let's do this."

"Good. My Realtor friend is going to meet us at the first building. Give me just a few more minutes to get ready, okay?"

"Take your time."

Melissa headed down a hallway. David did a quick once-over in a mirror near the front door, making sure he'd put himself together okay. He'd already put in four hours at the office that morning. Even though it was Sunday, and Thomas had suggested firm culture allowed for some freedom on that day, David couldn't risk falling behind Tidmore. He'd showered in a hurry and thrown on a pair of designer jeans and a brown sport coat. He felt like a zombie but didn't think he looked too bad.

The poodle, whom Melissa called Abby, kept him close company, hovering and sniffing around his ankles the entire time. Melissa's place was decorated to the nines, of course, and belonged in an interior design magazine.

When Melissa came back out of the bedroom, she somehow looked even more beautiful than she had a few minutes earlier. He told her how much he loved her home. She said the house was a graduation gift from her father—her parents lived only six blocks away. She acted like it wasn't that big of a deal. David tried not to act too stunned. But he figured, in this neighborhood, the house had probably cost her father over $1 million. That was one hell of a graduation gift. Melissa clearly came from a different world—one David had wanted to be a part of since he was a kid.

Stepping outside, Melissa locked the front door, turned, and then stared at the street.

"David, you can't be serious."

"What's wrong?"

"You can't possibly expect to take me out on a date in *that*?"

He followed her eyes, stared at his tired and dusty old truck sitting at the curb in all its full glory, and laughed. "You haven't lived until you've cruised around town in a ninety-nine Chevy Silverado, Melissa."

"Ha ha. Look, we're *not* driving around in that thing. You're a hot new associate at one of the most prestigious law firms in this city. That truck does not suit you anymore."

He shrugged. "Yeah, well, a new vehicle is definitely in my plans. I just haven't had any time. I've been cooped up in my office all day and night. You want to drive your car?"

"No, but let's make a detour on our way."

The general manager at Land Rover Austin, a man in his fifties wearing a black polo and jeans, met them outside the front doors of the dealership, even though the place was closed on Sundays. Melissa had called him on his personal cell phone. His name was Ted Ludwick, and he told David he'd been heading the dealership for the past ten years. Melissa had mentioned that Ted was good friends with her father, since her dad swapped vehicles yearly. They made small talk with Ted as he unlocked the building and turned on a few lights. David felt a bit embarrassed about bothering the man on his off day. But Ted reassured them both it was perfectly okay. The man seemed used to this kind of treatment from wealthy clients. And Melissa clearly belonged in that category.

Melissa knew exactly what she wanted David to drive. She asked Ted to show them all the new Range Rover Sports on the lot. There were dozens of them. As they roamed, Ted began listing off the luxuries: the refined leather, the exquisite woods, the automatic and high-tech this and that. They were certainly incredible vehicles. Melissa wanted David to test-drive a shiny black one. Once inside, she opened the sunroof, turned up the stereo, and rolled down the windows. David had to admit the SUV moved with incredible power and grace, so unlike his Chevy, which jarred him at every turn. Melissa kept insisting that he just *had* to get the car, even though he'd noticed the sticker price was a whopping $85,000.

Sitting on the expensive leather, his hands wrapped around the steering wheel, with Melissa damn near glowing in the seat next to him, David told Ted he'd take it. Melissa practically jumped for joy, throwing her arms around David like a giddy teenager. Ted said they could leave with the vehicle. He'd have the paperwork sent over to the firm the next day.

The Realtor's name was Barbie, of all things, and David felt that she looked the part with her perfect blonde hair, ridiculous high heels, and a diamond ring the size of a bowling ball on one of her thin fingers. She was in her forties, and the tan and makeup were caked on thick. Barbie talked a hundred miles an hour, and her cell phone rang every thirty seconds. She made David feel dizzy from the beginning. She said she'd helped another lawyer recently buy a new house on Lake Austin and casually mentioned it cost $3 million. Barbie called it a steal.

They'd already seen two high-rise apartments within a few blocks of the office. They were both beautiful buildings with beautiful people behind the concierge desks. They were also both incredibly expensive, with the smallest available one-bedroom unit going for $3,800 per month. The tiny garage apartment he'd rented in Palo Alto from the nice Korean lady had cost him only $500, with all utilities included. They were now standing inside the Austonian, which looked even more luxurious to David than the first two shiny buildings. David was about to tell Barbie to go find him something in the $1,000-a-month range when she let it slip that a Realtor friend of hers had just helped another newly hired H&K associate, William Tidmore, lease a unit on the thirty-first floor. David kept his mouth shut and rode up the elevator. Melissa reached over and held his hand on the way. They shared a smile.

On the thirty-third floor, Barbie opened the door to a 1,200 square foot one-bedroom unit that was fully furnished. David was immediately drawn to the floor-to-ceiling windows. The view was spectacular. With a look straight up the center of downtown, he was practically staring down onto the dome of the Texas Capitol building, sitting there in the middle of the city in all its pink granite splendor. Just beyond that, the sprawling campus of the University of Texas and the giant football stadium. The firm was only two blocks away. It would certainly be efficient.

Peeling his eyes away from the windows, he followed Barbie and Melissa around the rest of the condo and halfway listened as she described the immaculate countertops, the hardwood floors, and the spa-like bathroom features. The furniture was all contemporary and appropriately luxurious. A huge flat-screen TV hung on the wall in the living room. Not that he'd even have time to watch it. David shook his head. He was a hell of a long ways from the beat-up silver RV trailer back in Wink, Texas.

Barbie kept going on and on about the luxurious life of the Austonian. Tuning her out, David returned to the windows and the view. Melissa stepped up next to him, put her hand in his again as they stood there together. He had to admit this was all intoxicating. The glitz, the glamour, the prestige—the woman standing next to him. Everything he'd always wanted.

He thought of William Tidmore living below him.

"How much?" he asked Barbie.

"A bargain, David. Only six thousand a month."

He swallowed. It was a ridiculous amount of money. But his head was literally in the clouds. "I'll take it."

They had dinner at Eddie V's. Scallops, filet mignon, brussels sprouts, sautéed spinach, grilled asparagus, crab fried rice, and a bottle of wine. Melissa talked about her work at her father's financial firm and how she would take over from him one day. David was scarce with information about his own life. He mentioned getting a scholarship to play football in college before getting injured. He talked about working hard to get into a top law school and excelling while he was at Stanford. He mentioned mock trial championships, law school honors, the big-firm offers he'd gotten from across the country, and his decision to join Hunter & Kellerman. He did not talk about living in an RV while growing up, only wearing clothes purchased at garage sales, or the four months they had actually been homeless.

Melissa excused herself to go to the restroom. David took a moment to try and process everything that had happened today. He tried not to freak out about all the money he'd already committed himself to in his very first week at the firm. He should be fine. He knew as long as he kept working hard, putting in the hours, and hitting his numbers, the money would be there. Still, it was a bit of a shock to his system. But this was the life he'd wanted.

Melissa's phone buzzed on the table across from him. Looked like a text message. David wondered if maybe a girlfriend was checking in to see how her date was going. Out of curiosity, he reached over, picked up the phone, took a peek at the screen. He did a quick double take, stunned to find the name of his boss.

Marty Lyons: Any update?

David's brow bunched. Lyons? Melissa hadn't mentioned anything about knowing his boss. He quickly set the phone on the table when he spotted Melissa making her way back to their table from across the room. She settled back into her chair, and they continued to enjoy their meal together. David waited to find an opening to ask about Lyons. But he didn't want to come right out with it, as he'd have to admit he'd invaded her privacy by looking at her phone.

"Does your firm have any clients at Hunter and Kellerman?" he asked.

"A few. Jaworski, Mendohl, Tyndall, Lyons." She smiled. "Don't worry, David, I don't want your money. At least, not yet."

TEN

Charlie Nicks loved to drink Budweiser and watch old John Wayne movies while sitting in his filthy sweat-soaked recliner until he passed out drunk. It had become his nightly ritual over the past six months—ever since Hilda, his last live-in girlfriend, had moved out. He'd met Hilda when she was waiting tables at the Waffle House. She was nice enough. Decent on the eyes. Been divorced only twice. She'd taken pretty good care of him for a while. But Hilda eventually wanted to become wife number four, and Charlie was done with weddings, marriages, and everything else in between. At sixty-four, he felt it was a complete waste of time. Just made the end of the relationship more complicated. Hilda wanted to know why their relationship had to eventually end. Why couldn't they be together forever? This conversation had come up a lot in their last month together, to which Charlie usually replied, "Everything ends. One way or another. We're all just passing through this miserable life. Now go get me a beer."

Hilda had put up with him longer than the two gals before her. Neither of those old broads had lasted even three months. About two months had become pretty standard since Charlie's last divorce fifteen years ago. Most women couldn't handle his unique charm for much longer than that. He laughed at that thought as he grabbed his tenth beer of the night from the dirty fridge and stumbled back over to his brown recliner. The black mutt had decided to curl up in his chair while he was in the crapper. He pushed her away.

"Get out of here, Lucy! Go on, git!"

Falling into the recliner, Charlie found his glasses on the end table, slipped them on, and opened his beer. He leaned back and kicked up his bare feet as the recliner squeaked into position. With the remote, he turned the TV up to full volume. He didn't have too many neighbors to worry about bothering with the noise. His trailer was down a dirt road near a dumping ground. Although it wasn't prime property, Charlie liked it. He didn't want neighbors. He just wanted to be left the hell alone. One of his favorite flicks was on the tube tonight: *Rio Bravo*. It was hard to beat the Duke and Dean Martin together. He'd seen it probably a hundred times, and it never got old. Charlie took a swig. Dozens of empty and crumpled beer cans littered the table and the tattered carpet around the chair. He hadn't cleaned a damn thing since Hilda left.

He would clean the place one day. When he finally got lonely enough. There seemed to be plenty of old ladies out there who still wanted to feel needed by a man, even a loser like Charlie. In time, he would take a few garbage bags around his trailer, maybe pay the gal two trailers over a few bucks to spruce his place up a bit. He'd finally shower and shave, put on his best shirt and cowboy hat, and make his way down to the bar—see what broad he could convince that he was a good fixer-upper just waiting to happen. But he wouldn't lighten up on the drinking. He'd chosen Budweiser as his true bride a long time ago. Eventually, the gals all made the mistake of asking him about it. That was usually the beginning of the end.

Charlie saw a shadow move near the hallway bathroom.

"Stay out of the damn toilet, Lucy!" he yelled, his tongue starting to slur. Stupid dog was always drinking out of the toilet.

When his eyes started to drift, Charlie cursed himself. He wanted to stay awake long enough to see the last gunfight. He loved that damn scene. But he couldn't fight it. He was old and tired and drunk, and his body no longer had any willpower. He sensed more shadows in the living room with him but didn't even bother to look. Lucy was probably on the couch again. Hilda always hated that. He sure missed that old gal. Closing his eyes, he heard gunshots on the TV. His lips curled up at the corners. *Give 'em hell, Duke.*

Charlie was snoozing when the gun was placed to his head.

Sammy Diermont hiked the Garden Creek Falls trail on Casper Mountain every Friday morning at sunrise. The hike had been a staple of his exercise routine for nearly fifteen years. The hiking, biking, and swimming had kept him in better shape, even at sixty-three, than most of the younger agents who worked with him at his insurance office. The 2.5-mile trail was steep in different places, with wonderful rock formations. The view from the top was spectacular.

Sammy always took about twenty minutes to sit there at the top and reflect on his week. Lately, as he neared retirement age, he'd been thinking more and more about his blessed life. Three of their kids had stayed local. Sammy got to regularly see his nine energetic grandkids. Only his youngest son, Rick, had ventured to California. Rick was still single and trying to find himself. Sammy understood that—he'd joined the navy as a young man for the adventure. Still, Sammy had a feeling Rick would return one day, find himself a nice girl, and settle down to have a family. The strength of family always brought them back home to Casper. They all had a good life here.

On most Friday mornings, like today, Sammy had the summit to himself. Sitting on a rock, he took a moment to look out over the vast Wyoming landscape. God's country. He and his wife had moved to Casper forty years ago, right after Sammy had gotten out of the navy.

It'd been the best decision of their lives. Casper had been the perfect place to raise the kids. They were part of a small and caring community. His insurance business had thrived. When he retired in two years, he'd be turning his business over to his oldest son. What a blessing.

Sammy checked his heart rate, which, after the hard climb up, had now settled. It was time to start his descent down the mountain. After tightening the lace on a hiking boot, he began moving down the trail, his legs feeling extra spry today. He knew each and every nuance of the trail, where every sharp rock poked up, where to veer left or right, and where to be extra cautious. Turning a corner at brisk speed, Sammy almost bumped straight into a man. He was surprised he hadn't heard the man climbing up, but then Sammy's hearing had been failing him a lot lately. His wife kept wanting him to get it checked. The man in front of Sammy was young, probably in his late thirties, slender but muscular in his black T-shirt, hiking shorts, and boots. The man's hair was short and white. His face was hard, serious.

"Excuse me!" Sammy exclaimed.

"No problem," the man muttered, kept moving.

Sammy watched until the man disappeared around the boulder. He'd never seen the guy on the trail before. He had a strange feeling about him. After thirty-five years selling insurance, Sammy had learned to read people pretty well. The eyes told a lot about the soul of a person—they truly were a window. Sammy didn't like what he saw in the window of this guy. There was something hollow behind his gray eyes. He shrugged it off. Everyone has their struggles; it was not his place to pass judgment. He kept climbing down the mountain, pausing only briefly when he came upon a steep cliff with a more than fifty-foot drop. It was yet another wonderful view back over the town.

The push was quiet but fierce. Sammy felt the pressure of a hand on his back, but it was too late to respond. His hearing had completely failed him this morning. As he toppled over the cliff, Sammy realized there was more than just a struggle behind the white-haired man's hollow gray eyes. There was pure evil.

Marvin Shobert was at the horse track again. Lone Star Park was fifteen minutes from his home just outside Dallas. At first, the quick drive seemed like a blessing. Marvin could easily meet up with drinking buddies without drawing the ire of his wife, Brenda; however, the close proximity had become a curse the past few years as the gambling grew out of control and the debt choked him. Several times Marvin had been on the verge of climbing out of the financial pit, only to risk everything going for the *big* one, and had dug himself an even deeper hole.

Over the past few months, that hole had turned into the Grand Canyon. Marvin was desperate. He owed a hell of a lot of money to Jersey, a guy he'd been introduced to a year ago through one of his work buddies. As a bookie, Jersey was a nice-enough guy—but he worked for a much more sinister boss who wasn't nearly as forgiving. Two thugs had visited Marvin at the printer company a week ago. Right inside his office, they'd made serious threats and really scared him, along with a few coworkers. Marvin owed them $25,000. If he didn't pull it together within ten days, people were going to start getting hurt.

Marvin hadn't slept since that day. Brenda was concerned. He was pale and had the shakes. She kept asking him about his health and wanted him to go see a doctor. He assured his wife that he was fine, just simple work stress. Give it a few days. He hoped this would be true after tonight. He planned to turn $3,000 into more than $25,000 on one bet. Marvin had a good lead horse. The odds were right. He'd done thorough research. Hell, that's all he'd done the past two days in the office while avoiding all sales calls.

Marvin had a really good feeling about this one. After all, the horse was named Set Free. And that's all Marvin wanted to be right now. After tonight, he swore he'd be done with the track. The thrill was not worth the stress he'd been living with for months now. This time, it would be different. He was tired of living with the shame, too. The $3,000 he'd used for tonight's bet had been stolen from his eighty-four-year-old mother. He'd actually forged a check when visiting her in the assisted-living facility yesterday. A sixty-one-year-old man stealing money from his elderly mother. Shameful. But he hadn't been able to look at himself in the mirror for a long time now.

Tonight would change everything. He'd win the money back and replace it in her bank account like nothing had ever happened. Then he'd get the thugs off his back and take up a new hobby. Probably golf. It was hard to gamble much on golf—although Marvin knew you could gamble on just about anything.

The horse race tonight was not local. Marvin was watching it in the simulcast TV lounge with a bunch of other local gamblers. Sweating something fierce, he stood in the very back of the room. He'd actually said a prayer when he'd placed the bet. *God, just this one time.* How many gambling addicts had said that same prayer? He really meant it.

Watching the dozen TV screens in the front of the room, Marvin felt sick to his stomach. The race was about to start. He clenched his ticket in his fist. Set Free was out quickly. That was good—the horse didn't get caught up in the gate. Marvin held his breath. His horse was sitting third around the first turn, just four lengths back. He tried to swallow the thick knot stuck in his throat. His horse got caught by two other horses on the back stretch. Cursing, Marvin took a step toward the TV screens. His chest was so tight. He wondered if he might have a heart attack. If he didn't win this race, he might as well be dead, anyway. Set Free was running fifth at the final turn but still within striking distance. Marvin started to get dizzy. It wasn't looking good. *God, please.* Then Set Free caught a wind and quickly passed three other horses down the final stretch. His horse was only one length back from the leader and gaining ground.

"Come on!" Marvin yelled at the TVs. He was normally a quiet and reserved man, so the outburst caught him off guard. Others in the lounge were also screaming at the TVs. It was all part of the fun and excitement, although Marvin doubted anyone else in the room had as much on the line as he did.

The horses were nearing the finish line. Set Free was still gaining on the leader, just a head back. It would be so damn close. Marvin held his breath as the horses blasted through the finish. He stared frozen at the TV screens, waiting for the official results. When they flashed on the screen, he realized his horse had actually won. Marvin couldn't believe his eyes. He'd done it. He'd actually done it. A few others in the room cursed at the TVs while a couple of guys started high-fiving. Marvin couldn't move—he stood perfectly still, his body numb. Set Free had actually won.

Seconds later, all the emotion of the moment hit Marvin at once, and he became physically nauseated. He was going to vomit. Rushing around the corner of the lounge, he found the hallway to the men's restroom. He grabbed a stall, shut the door behind him, and dropped to his knees on the dirty floor. He then proceeded to spew his dinner and drinks into the toilet in one violent upheaval. Finished, he tried to catch his breath. His old body just couldn't handle the intense nerves anymore. He quickly flushed the toilet so as not to stare at his own vomit, but continued to kneel while trying to somehow gather himself again.

He felt like celebrating. He'd have enough cash left over for another race. Just one for the road before he let it all go for good. He quickly caught himself, realizing how stupid he was. Shaking his head, he decided he'd cash out his ticket and get the hell out of there as fast as possible. He'd been given one last pass at life, and he wasn't going to spoil it. *Thank you, Lord.*

He heard footsteps in the quiet restroom outside his stall. Then the door handle for his stall was pulled against the latch. "Someone's in here," Marvin muttered, still breathing heavily. Odd, since there were five other open stalls available.

Another yank on his stall door.

"Hey!" Marvin exclaimed. "I said I'm using this one!"

When his stall door burst open, all Marvin saw were the gray eyes of the young man before the back of his hair was grabbed in a ruthless fist and his face was shoved down into the toilet water. Marvin tried to struggle but felt powerless against the strength of the man. He wanted to shout, *Wait! I have your money!* But nothing would come out in the gurgle of water he was now swallowing.

Seconds later, his body stopped convulsing as his mind went to a different place altogether. All Marvin could think about was his winning horse.

Set Free. How appropriate.

ELEVEN

David billed the most hours of anyone in the firm's history during his first month with Hunter & Kellerman. For a seventy-one-year-old law firm, it was a phenomenal feat. Everyone was stunned. Marty Lyons and the other partners told the litigation group they'd reviewed David's billing entries exhaustively, just to be certain—everything checked out. David had broken a billing record set by Lyons himself more than twenty years ago. Only a month into his legal career, David was clearly the firm's newest superstar. Lyons and the other partners celebrated him with full accolades at the litigation group's monthly meeting. David felt awkward. It was clear most of the associates despised him for his achievement, as it only raised the level of pressure and expectation on all of them. But they all engaged in the necessary cheering, clapping, and backslapping when Lyons made the toast. *All hail David Adams!*

Tidmore seemed defeated. Although they'd been neck and neck in the beginning, David had run away with the victory the final two weeks—with a little help from an old friend. David told himself it was only temporary. He just needed a little something *extra* to keep his eyes open and focused in the dark hours of the night, when everyone else had gone home. Plus, Melissa had proved to be a powerful force of nature. She'd been regularly pulling David out of the office to show him off at fancy dinners with important people. David had to somehow make up for the lost time—the only way to do that was to work through the night. It was the same thing he'd told himself during his second year at Stanford. A little something extra went a long way to help him to study, go to class, participate in mock trials, and cover enough shifts at the Dutch Goose to somehow afford to stay in school.

The former classmate who had introduced him to the small blue pills had called them Uncle Billy. He always said, "Let Uncle Billy help you out." Call them whatever—Billy, whiz, speed, uppers, goey, louee—they gave David the added edge he needed to skip sleep, stay alert, stay focused, stay at the office all night, and get the job done to a spectacularly new level. His former classmate, who'd dropped out of law school altogether, had shipped a supply to David from California. David could afford a lot more of them now. With Uncle Billy's help, he'd managed to keep both Melissa and Lyons happy with him.

The day after the toast, Lyons moved David into the more spacious office directly next to the partner's corner power suite. Another awkward moment for David was passing the fourth-year associate in the hallway who'd been downgraded and moved out. David shrugged it off—it was all part of the game. Hell, everyone knew the high stakes of what they'd signed up for. With an arm around his shoulder, Lyons told David he wanted his protégé close by. The future was bright. Before he left David's office, Lyons placed an envelope on his desk and said the partners had all agreed on a special bonus for his incredible achievement. When Lyons left, David opened the envelope and found a bonus check for $5,000.

David peered up from his desk when Thomas entered his new office, shut the door behind him, and then stood there, arms crossed, eyes narrow.

"What?" David asked.

"What the hell are you doing?"

"What do you mean? Working on your brief."

"I'm not talking about that." Thomas stepped closer to the desk, keeping his voice at a volume that couldn't be heard outside the office. "You have to slow down, David. You're going to wreck yourself. No attorney should ever bill as much as you did last month. It's impossible to put in that kind of work *and* stay healthy."

"I'm fine, Thomas."

"Tell that to your face," Thomas chided him. "Your eyes are red, and your cheeks look gaunt. You've probably already lost ten pounds since you got here."

"I needed to drop ten, anyway," David quipped, forcing a grin.

Thomas sighed. "This isn't a joke. Have you learned nothing from Nick's suicide? If you don't take your foot off the accelerator soon, you're going to crash and burn your first year."

"I haven't heard Lyons voicing any concerns."

"And you never will, believe me. But I'm not Lyons."

"Look, I said I'm fine, okay?"

Thomas shook his head. "Please just take what I'm saying under consideration."

"All right, I hear you already."

After finishing up another long day at work, David cut through an alley on his walk home late that night. He was so tired, he could barely walk straight. Although he'd tried to reassure Thomas he was okay, David knew he was not. There was no way he could keep up with this pace. He was already popping twice as many blue pills as he had back in law school. His dealer had actually asked him if he was selling to other lawyers. David assured the guy he was simply storing them away for future use. After getting off the phone, he'd cursed himself. Was he seriously lying to a damn drug dealer? What the hell was wrong with him? Was he going to end up like Nick, with a rope around his neck?

He stepped around a dumpster, careful to avoid several muddy puddles left over from a rain shower earlier that afternoon. He was looking down, watching his steps, so as not to get his brand-new dress shoes wet, when he felt someone step out in front of him. David stopped, startled. The man looked to be in his twenties, with a tough-guy goatee, and he wore a dirty white tank top that showed every square inch of his muscled arms covered in tattoos. David could make out a red dragon tattoo that looked like it was hissing fire up the man's neck. This was not someone you wanted to encounter in a dark alley.

"Yo, dude, you got a smoke?" the guy said.

"Sorry, don't smoke."

David tried to quickly sidestep the guy and keep on moving, but the dragon shifted over to block his path. David cursed. They were only a few feet away from each other now. He thought he could smell a mix of alcohol and marijuana on the guy. This was not good. He was standing alone in a damn alley with a guy who looked like he wanted to break David in half. A man who was clearly not interested in David simply walking away from him right now.

"Then how about you buy me some smokes?" the thug snarled.

"Look, man, I'm just trying to get home."

David heard it before he spotted it. The familiar click of a switchblade. He used to play with his friend Joey's knife back in the sixth grade. Peering down, he spotted the shiny, sharp object in the man's right hand. David felt another wave of fear race up his back and tighten his muscles. Could this really be happening? Would the firm have to deal with back-to-back deaths of two lawyers? He was suddenly envisioning headlines about the bright young attorney destined for greatness who got stabbed to death in an alley. The partners would mourn him— there went their future cash cow. Tidmore would throw a private party.

"Okay, settle down," David stammered. "I got some cash. You can have it."

"I want *everything*."

"Fine. Just be cool, okay?"

David began to slowly reach into his pockets, searching for his wallet, as well as his keys. He couldn't be certain handing over his valuables would be enough to satisfy this guy. He still might have to protect himself if this thug didn't want to leave him unharmed. He grabbed his wallet from his right pocket with his right hand. With his left, he found his condo key, squeezed it tightly in his palm. A switchblade versus a condo key. It was nowhere near a fair fight, but it was all he had on him. The dragon was watching him closely, the switchblade now raised in front of him. Adrenaline coursed through David. Sweat poured down his back. He felt his whole life flash before him. All the hard work. All the damn studying and the countless hours of sacrifice. He'd *finally* arrived. And now, in this moment, if he wasn't careful, everything could be taken away from him.

A shadow of another man suddenly appeared right behind the dragon. David never even noticed the second guy—neither did the muscle-bound freak. An arm went around the dragon's neck and yanked him backward in a fierce choke hold. The dragon gasped for air, stunned by the sudden sneak attack, his eyes bulging. The dragon began whipping around, trying to grab the man and sling him off. But the shadow guy only squeezed harder around the dragon's neck. When it was clear to the dragon that he was not going to be able to toss the man aside, he changed tactics and instead slammed them both up against a metal dumpster as hard as he could. The shadow guy's head collided violently against the dumpster, causing him to release the dragon. Gaining his freedom, the tattooed guy in the tank top stumbled forward, gasping for air and clutching at his neck.

Standing there, David was unsure what he should do next. Should he run for it? Or should he now jump on the guy himself? He turned around when he heard loud noises in the alley behind him. David spotted a group of college guys, all laughing and whooping it up as if they'd just enjoyed a raucous night on the town. However, they stopped when they realized they were walking in on something bad going down. The dragon also noticed the guys and decided it was time for him to clear out. He turned and staggered out the opposite end of the alley. The frat guys also backtracked, leaving David now standing there alone with the stranger who'd just saved his life. The man had slumped all the way down to the wet concrete and was leaning against the dumpster.

Kneeling, David got his first good look at the face of the man. He shook his head, stunned. An old homeless guy who was probably in his seventies. His face was dirty and unshaven; his clothes smelled of sweat and body odor. He wore a black trench coat, dark pants, and unlaced brown work boots. The old man wasn't moving. Had he been knocked out cold? David could tell the man was still breathing, so that was good. At least he wasn't already dead. Looking closer, David could see a trail of blood trickling down the back of the man's neck. The collision with the metal dumpster had done some real damage.

Standing again, David looked both ways up and down the alley, wondering what the hell to do next. His first selfish instinct was to just get the hell out of there and get on with his life. He really didn't want to have to deal with something like this right now. However, David couldn't just leave him there. The guy had put his own life on the line. David thought of calling the cops but knew that would only create a much bigger mess for him to have to manage. He just needed to help the guy recover a bit. Get him patched up, maybe give him some food or something.

The old guy suddenly opened his eyes, moaned a bit.

"Hey, man," David said, kneeling again. "You okay?"

Another moan as the guy shifted. The man's eyes were open but unfocused. He was dazed and confused. The old man tried to push himself up off the concrete, but then his eyes rolled back, and he slumped over to the side. David caught him before he fell straight on his face. The guy seemed to be out cold again. Steadying the man, David got a much better look at the back of his head. There was definitely a gash, but overall, it didn't look too bad. It didn't necessarily warrant a trip to the ER.

The guy woke up again, tried to get up but failed. Reaching down, David wrapped the man's arm around his shoulder and then lifted him up off the pavement. With his other hand, he grabbed the guy's waist and held on to him, like a teammate helping an injured friend gradually hobble off the football field.

"Come on, buddy," David said.

Making their way out onto the main sidewalk, David guided the man two blocks over toward the front entrance of the Austonian. He wondered what kind of stares he would get as he dragged a dirty, bleeding homeless guy through the building's pristine lobby. He was about to find out. Pushing through the glass doors, he recognized Josh, the twentysomething concierge behind the front counter. Josh gave him a curious look.

"Everything okay, sir?" Josh asked.

"Yep. Things just got a little wild tonight."

David kept moving before Josh could say anything else. He hit an elevator button, waited, looked at the guy he held in his arms again. The man's head hung down in front of him. He looked pretty much out of it. When the elevator doors parted, a group of pretty girls dressed for the bars stepped out, then stopped and glared at David and his friend.

"Evening, ladies," David said, smiling, pushing right past them.

He quickly pressed a button, watched the doors shut. He was making quite the impression around the building. Minutes later, they were finally inside his swank condo on the thirty-third floor. The homeless guy moaned and shifted every few seconds. David dragged him into his bedroom, grabbed several towels from his bathroom, tried to spread them out on his new plush bed, then carefully lowered the old guy on top.

Sunk into the cushion of the bed, the guy was quickly out again. Turning on a bedside lamp, David stood over the man. He ran his fingers through his hair, trying to sort out what the hell to do next. From the bathroom, he grabbed a hand towel, soaked it in warm water from the sink, and then returned to the man. He turned the man's head to get a better look at his wound. Fortunately, it had stopped bleeding, which was good, but there was still *a lot* of sticky blood along with all sorts of other dirt and street grime. David began dabbing at the man's head with the wet towel and tried to clean up the wound. He completely soiled one towel and grabbed a fresh one to finish the job.

Beneath the sink, he found a first-aid kit. Opening it, he pulled out a roll of gauze, some medical tape, and a tube of antibiotic ointment. Upon close inspection of the wound, he guessed the guy was suffering more from concussion symptoms than the actual gash, as it really wasn't too bad. David had suffered two concussions back in his football days. A serious hit to the head for an old man like this could put him out for a good bit. David did his best amateur medic job and patched up the wound with the gauze and medical tape.

Standing over the bed again, David took another close look at the man's weathered face. There were deep lines and wrinkles, probably from being out in the direct sun too much. He noticed several scars all over the man's balding head and one long one running behind his left ear down his neck. The guy had really been through it in his lifetime. Beneath the dirty black trench coat, the old guy wore a worn-out Texas Longhorns T-shirt. The pants were dark-blue Dockers and had holes in both knees. The work boots were in decent shape.

David wondered if the man had any ID on him. Who was this guy? Why had he put his own life on the line in the alley? The man had started to snore, so David didn't worry too much about waking him. He began searching his coat pockets. He found an assortment of goods from a life most likely on the streets. The trench-coat pockets held a bottle of water, a roll of napkins, a granola bar, an apple, a battered John Grisham novel, and what looked like a half-eaten peanut butter sandwich in a resealable bag. In one pants pocket, he found a few wadded-up dollar bills and a collection of spare change. In the other pocket, he pulled out a pack of cigarettes and a small pocket-size Bible. David didn't find *any* ID on the man. He also didn't find any remnants of drugs or alcohol, which surprised him.

Returning the items, David tried to help the guy get as comfortable as possible. He carefully pulled off the work boots, revealing the dirtiest pair of white socks he'd ever seen in his life. About half the toes poked out of holes, all of them looking battered and bruised. One toenail was red with pus and looked like it was badly infected. David practically gagged.

Then David noticed a bulge under the top of one of his socks. Pulling the sock down, he discovered an envelope with a black *X* on the outside. When he opened the envelope to peek inside, David was stunned. There was *a lot* of cash. Brand-new $100 bills. He pulled the cash out and quickly skimmed it. David cursed, stared back at the face of the old guy. Thousands of dollars? What the hell? Had the guy robbed a bank?

Returning the cash to the envelope, David again stuffed it under the man's dirty sock where he'd found it. He turned off the bedside lamp and left the bedroom. In the kitchen, he poured himself a glass of cold water and quickly downed it, tried to collect himself. Again, he shook his head, couldn't believe all that had transpired that evening.

Checking his watch, David quickly worked up a plan. He decided he'd hang out on the sofa in the living room for a few hours and allow the guy to sleep it off in the bedroom. Then he'd get him up, let him shower if he wanted, maybe give him some new clothes, wish him the best, and send him on his merry way. David could still be at H&K by six the next morning.

The plan failed when he couldn't wake the guy. David tried at two in the morning. A few nudges on the man's shoulder, a few "Hey, buddy, come on, wake up already," but the guy wouldn't stir. He just kept snoring away like a freight train. David tried again at three. Nothing. He tried again at four, this time with full-volume talking. No luck. David didn't quite have the heart to shake him awake. So from four to seven, David lay on his sofa—one clearly designed more for its modern look than comfort—and basically stared at his bedroom doorway, waiting for the guy to appear.

At seven, David gave up. He got himself cleaned up and dressed for the office. Hell, the old guy could sleep it off all day if he wanted. Just as long as he was gone when David returned. He grabbed a notepad and pen and scribbled a brief note that he left on the bed next to the man. David wrote the last sentence as his way of implying he didn't expect to see the homeless guy still sitting in his condo when he got back.

Friend, thank you for what you did for me last night. Please feel free to use the shower. You'll find some extra clothes by the sink, if you want them, including several pairs of brand-new socks. Help yourself to whatever you want in the kitchen. Good luck to you. —David

TWELVE

Around noon, David called the Austonian and asked the concierge on duty if she happened to have seen an older man wearing a black trench coat and work boots carrying a big flat-screen TV out of the building. The concierge had not and seemed confused by his question. David reassured her everything was fine. But he wondered if the old man was still there.

Early that evening, David decided to pop in to his condo just to check on things. He half expected to find his new homeless friend plopped down on the sofa, a bag of chips in his lap, *SportsCenter* on the TV. But when David walked into the condo, the old man was gone. The bed was made up perfectly, not a wrinkle in it. Peeking into the bathroom, David found everything nice and tidy, even more so than when he'd left for work that morning. David noticed a towel had been folded neatly on the bathroom counter—the guy had at least showered. The socks were also gone. Then David found a message from the guy scribbled beneath the note David had left for him that morning.

Thank you for the shower and the clothes. I'll be at Caroline's tonight. How about I buy you a meal? —Benny

Caroline's was a popular dining spot a few blocks from the firm. After walking over to the restaurant, David spotted Benny at a table near the back all by himself. It was a weeknight, and the restaurant was only a third full. The ragged old man wore the same black trench coat, same work boots. David wondered if he was wearing the new socks he'd given him. He watched as a waitress came over, gave Benny a glass of soda, patted him warmly on the back, and seemed genuinely happy to see him. David thought about what to talk about with the man. It wasn't like they had a lot in common. *Where'd you learn a choke hold like the one you performed in the alley? Where the hell did all that cash in your sock come from?*

Benny was reading something at the table—it looked like the small Bible he'd had in his coat pocket. The waitress delivered a sandwich and some fries to him. She again patted Benny on the back. David figured the man must be a welcome regular in the place, which he found interesting.

Feeling like a coward, David finally walked over to the old man's table.

"Benny?" he said.

Benny looked up from his food, his eyes softening as he seemed to recognize David. "Well, well, if it's not the man who patched me up and got me back on my feet." He smiled wide, showing tobacco-stained teeth.

"How's your head?" David asked.

"Good as new, thanks to you."

"Glad to hear it."

"Please join me. Sit down," Benny offered. "I'm glad you came." David slid into the booth across from him.

"You a doctor?" Benny asked, taking a bite of his chicken sandwich.

"Hardly. A lawyer. My name's David."

"Like the shepherd," Benny replied.

David tilted his head. "Sorry?"

Benny smiled again, pointed at the small Bible sitting on the table. "From the Scriptures. David was a shepherd. First, with the animals. Eventually, he was a shepherd to God's people. You have a distinguished name, my friend."

David shrugged. "I guess. But I'm no shepherd."

"Not yet, maybe." Another smile. The man smiled a lot. "I wanted to properly thank you for letting me stay with you last night."

"No, it's me who should be thanking you, Benny."

"You already did, Shep. That was the best shower I've had in months."

"A shower is hardly proper thanks for a man who saved my life."

Benny waved it off. "Nah, I was just in the right place at the right time."

"Why'd you do it, anyway? You could've been killed yourself."

Benny shrugged again. "At least I'd have died doing the right thing, Shep."

David noted it was the second time Benny had called him *Shep*. He figured it was because of the whole shepherd in the Bible thing. Didn't matter much to David. After saving his life, the old man could call him whatever the hell he wanted.

"I'm serious, Benny. How can I help you? Do you need something?"

David figured the invite to dinner was because the guy might want more financial help. And David was willing to give it—within reason.

"I have everything I need. But if you're going to keep carrying on, how about you buy me a piece of blueberry cobbler from Rosie over there, and we'll call it even. Deal?"

David grinned. There was something about the old man and that perpetually crooked-toothed smile. Benny either held the keys to peace, or he was as crazy as a loon. David wasn't sure yet. He was guessing the latter.

"Blueberry cobbler, huh? You got it. I'll have a piece, too."

They ordered two pieces of blueberry cobbler with vanilla ice cream from the waitress, who quickly brought their dessert back over to the table. Both David and the old man grabbed spoons and went to work.

"So . . . you're a lawyer?" Benny asked.

"Yeah, for about a month now."

"You like being a lawyer?"

David thought about it for a second. "I'm not really sure yet, to be honest."

"You keep people out of jail?"

"No, not really. My firm defends big companies who are getting sued by other big companies."

"Sounds important."

David shrugged. "It pays the bills."

"Ha! I'd say it does a lot more than that. You got yourself a really nice place, my friend. I didn't even know they made beds that comfortable. Almost didn't want to go home after staying there with you."

"You have a home, Benny?" David asked, just kind of stupidly blurting it out.

Benny frowned. "You think I'm homeless or something, Shep?"

"I didn't mean it that way . . . sorry . . . I just . . ."

Benny laughed it off. "I'm messing with you, son. It's okay, I know how I look." He wiped cobbler from his mouth with a napkin. "Sure, I got my own place. Can't exactly get my mail delivered there or watch satellite TV, I'll admit, but it's a safe place to go each night and put my head on a pillow. Which should never be taken for granted."

David thought about the months he'd slept in a van as a kid. "You're right."

Benny set his fork down, smiled wide. "Hey, you want to see it?"

"Your home?"

Benny shrugged. "Sure, why not? I figure you invited me into *your* home, showed me some real good hospitality. The least I could do is return the favor."

David pondered the invite for a moment. He really needed to get back to the office; he had so much work to do. His desk was piled high with papers. However, the thought of that felt really depressing at the moment. Tonight, he'd rather go check out Benny's cardboard box under some bridge—or *wherever* the man stayed each night.

"Sure, Benny, let's go see your home."

THIRTEEN

When Benny mentioned they'd need to catch several different city bus routes that would eventually get them over to his place on the east side of town, David offered to drive them instead. He walked back to the Austonian, retrieved his SUV, and then picked up Benny along the curb outside Caroline's. Once inside the Range Rover, Benny stared wide-eyed at the fancy computer screen in the dash.

"You know what all these buttons do?" Benny asked.

"Not really."

"Looks like a fighter-jet cockpit. They give out these to all the new lawyers over at Hunter and Kellerman?"

David cocked his head. Had he mentioned the name of his firm to the old man?

"Something like that," David said.

"Then I might have to go back to law school." Benny cackled.

David smiled. "Stanford could use a guy like you."

"That where they taught you how to be a lawyer?"

David thought of the blue pills. "Yes, among other things."

David crossed under I-35 and headed into East Austin, where they drove through a unique mix of crack alleys and urban gentrification, depending on the block. Benny pointed him this way and that as they navigated farther away from downtown.

"What about you, Benny? You go to school?"

"School of hard knocks. Spent eight years in the navy."

"That where they taught you to put a choke hold on a man?"

Benny looked over, nodded. "Yes, sir, among other things."

Taking a left down a side street, David drove them into a low-income neighborhood with dimly lit streets filled with small, mismatched old houses. Most of them looked like they were on their last legs. They drove past some rough-looking people who were hanging out on porches and in driveways. Men who looked a lot like the dragon dude who'd pulled the knife on him in the alley. The Range Rover got some serious stares. Fidgeting in his leather seat, David hoped the old man knew where the hell he was taking him. He didn't feel like getting himself shot on this journey. He looked over and noticed Benny in the passenger seat kind of mumbling to himself as he gazed out the window. *Crazy as a loon,* David thought.

"Right over there, Shep," Benny said, pointing up ahead. "You can park on the curb."

David eased his car to the curb in front of a decent-looking one-story white brick house that sat at the end of the street next to a thick set of woods. David studied the house, quite surprised. The yard was mowed and well maintained. There was a front porch with two rockers. It was not at all what he expected.

"This is nice, Benny," David said, staring at the house.

Benny laughed. "We're not quite there yet. Come on. We walk from here."

David turned, brow wrinkled. Walk? The street had dead-ended. There were no more houses. He got out of the Range Rover, made sure it was locked, and joined Benny in the middle of the street. Benny said to follow him closely. They walked to the end of the street and stepped into the tall grass headed toward the woods. David wasn't sure what to think. Benny lived in the woods? David didn't say anything, just kept following the mumbling old man.

Pulling out a small flashlight from his coat pocket, Benny found a narrow walking trail. As they began stepping through the first set of trees, it quickly became dark along the trail, although Benny seemed to know exactly where he was going. He moved at a steady pace, in and around trees, down a small hill, up another, and through a brief clearing.

As instructed, David stayed close to the old man—although he began to wonder if he was about to be led out to the middle of nowhere and be cut into a hundred pieces. This was creepy as hell. Still wearing his dress slacks, button-down shirt, and shiny black shoes, David wasn't exactly dressed for a night of hiking through the woods. He wanted to turn the hell around but didn't have the heart to tell Benny, since the old man seemed excited. Benny slowed when a noise pushed through some branches up ahead. David felt his pulse quicken. They'd probably already traveled more than a hundred yards. What the hell was out here? Using his flashlight, Benny plodded forward again along the trail.

"Watch your step here," Benny suggested.

They crossed over a small creek. Someone had created a makeshift bridge of sorts with several two-by-fours nailed together.

"We almost there, Benny?"

"Yep. Just down this next hill and around Mikey's Turn."

Mikey's Turn? David felt completely lost. If the old man somehow ditched him or had a heart attack, David would probably never find his way back to the street. As they hiked down a small hill, David heard another rustling ahead of them, sending a chill through him. Then they were suddenly blinded by a bright light.

"Put that down, Curly!" Benny said.

"Sorry, Benny," said a voice behind the light. "Who's that with you?"

"A friend. He's okay."

The bright light lowered. Benny led David up to a guy wearing a denim jacket and blue jeans. The man was sitting in a cheap lawn chair next to the path. With rough gray stubble on his chin and cheeks, he looked to be in his forties. It was easy for David to see why Benny called the man Curly, as he had a wild mop of thick, curly brown hair. David wondered why the man was sitting in a lawn chair by this path. Was he a lookout or something?

"How are you, Benny?" Curly asked, standing and hugging the old man.

"Real good. You?"

"All right."

"You get that job with the roofer?"

Curly nodded with a smile. "Yessir. Two steady weeks of work starting on Tuesday."

"That's great. We're all proud of you."

"Thank you, sir."

Benny turned back to David. "This is my friend, Shep."

Curly nodded politely. "How do you do, sir?"

"I'm fine, thank you."

"Watch your step these last fifty yards," Curly suggested. "It gets a little steep, and it looks like you don't have great shoes for it."

"Thanks, I'll be careful. Good to meet you."

"You, too, Shep."

Benny led David up the path another fifty yards until they turned and suddenly entered a large clearing in the middle of the woods. David could hear music up ahead. It sounded like someone was playing a guitar. Several voices were singing. As they moved deeper into the clearing, David could see the light of a large campfire with about a dozen men sitting and standing all around it. A man in the middle was indeed playing the guitar. To the right of the campfire, David noticed a huge canopy propped up with lanterns hanging underneath—it looked like some kind of makeshift kitchen. As they drew closer, David could see a couple of guys preparing food. Beyond that, David spotted several camping tents—more than twenty of them.

David was mesmerized. "What the hell is this, Benny?"

Benny turned, smiled wide. "Welcome to the Camp. My home."

"You live . . . here?"

"Yep. Come on, I'll introduce you to everyone."

As they stepped into the full light of the campfire, the guitarist paused his playing and damn near everyone looked over toward David, making him feel uneasy. Was this the part of the horror movie where the zombies all attacked and ate him?

"Boys, meet Shep," Benny announced. "He's a friend of the Camp."

With Benny's introduction, nearly everyone suddenly jumped up and rushed over to greet David, hands thrust at him, lots of guys patting him on the back, saying hello, welcome, and introducing themselves, all in a flurry of activity. David met Elvis, a thirtysomething guy with long black hair, sideburns, and wearing a dirty Dallas Cowboys cap. He met Larue, a young black man with cornrows who should probably still be in high school. There was Shifty, a man probably older than Benny, with wisps of white hair on his head but with half his teeth clearly missing. That didn't stop Shifty from constantly smiling. Doc, a beanpole of a man in his fifties, wore a flannel button-down and khaki slacks and looked like he could be a college professor. What was Doc doing out here? David met about a dozen other interesting characters, unable to keep all their names and faces straight, the welcomes coming so fast and furious—men of all colors, ages, and physical makeups. It was about the friendliest bunch of guys he'd ever met.

As they all eased back over to their camping chairs, David turned to Benny.

"They all live *here*, Benny?"

"Yessir. Make yourself comfortable."

The guitarist, a man called Red, most likely because of the color of his long hair, picked his instrument up and began playing again.

David recognized the tune from the days his mother had dragged him to church. "The Old Rugged Cross." Red began to sing, "On a hill far away . . ." and without hesitation, half the men joined right in with him at full volume. David smiled at the sight. They weren't bad singers, either, for a misfit choir of homeless guys—although David guessed he couldn't really call them all that. They had a home—sort of.

David wandered over toward the kitchen canopy. Two men were whipping up a stew of sorts, cutting up stacks of vegetables and dropping them into a large pot. One of them mentioned to David that dinner would be ready in about ten minutes.

Shifty, the old white-haired man with all the missing teeth, grabbed David by the arm. "You want the grand tour, Shep?"

David shrugged. "Sure, thanks."

Shifty led David down a lantern-lit trail toward the camping tents. He stopped near the first four tents that were all bunched in a tight circle.

"These belong to the elders," Shifty mentioned.

"Who are the elders?"

"Doc, Mulligan, Walter, and Benny."

"How did they become elders?"

"Doc and Mulligan founded the Camp. Walter and Benny were voted in by the boys a few years ago."

Shifty pushed ahead, as the trail led to another circle with about ten more tents. Shifty explained that these tents all belonged to the regulars—guys who'd already been through the program and had kept the covenant. Shifty showed off his own home—a standard, brown three-man camping tent. Shifty said he'd recently upgraded from a two-man tent and now had a ton of room for all his things. Inside, David noted a sleeping bag and pillow, a black duffel bag stuffed with clothes, and a basket that held books and other assorted items. Shifty seemed really proud of his tent. It was about half the size of David's closet.

Continuing the tour, Shifty tugged David down a slight hill, where he noticed that two large blue tarps had been hung between two trees, like makeshift walls.

"The shower," Shifty explained.

"Where do you get water?" David asked, assuming there was no plumbing.

Shifty smiled wide again. The man was missing both front teeth. It was quite the sight. He pointed to the sky. "From the good man upstairs. We collect rain in two barrels. Doc created a pulley system to use the water for showering. Works pretty good. Better than soaping up in the restroom at McDonald's, I'll tell you that."

"I see."

David now knew why Benny had considered the shower in his condo such a treat. Moving past the showers, they circled back up the hill toward the campfire again. Shifty walked him over to a small clearing, where four long wooden benches had been placed that all faced a hand built five foot wooden cross.

"This here is the chapel," Shifty said. "We do church here three times a week. Both Doc and Benny preach a pretty good sermon."

The final section was a small circle of four one-man tents.

"Whose tents are these?" David asked, wondering what was next.

"They're for the freshmen. Guys who've just entered the program. They stay here until they've fulfilled all the steps. Then they can move over with the regulars, like me."

"What all do you do in the program?"

"First off, get sober and stay clean. No drugs or alcohol are allowed in the Camp. That's the first thing that'll get you suspended. You also start giving regularly to the community fund. Not much, just a tiny portion of any earnings. We take care of each other. You learn a new trade or polish up an old one through one of the classes offered at the different ministries in town. You attend chapel regularly. And you meet with your mentor every other day."

"How long is this program?"

"Six months."

"Sounds pretty hard-core."

"Well, it's hard-core to live out on the streets."

David nodded. "How long have you been here, Shifty?"

Another big smile from the man. "Two years already. Haven't touched a drop of alcohol in seven hundred eleven days. Thank you, Jesus."

After completing the tour, they returned to the other men, who were still sitting around the campfire. Bowls of stew were being passed out to everyone. Red launched into "How Great Thou Art." One of the men whom David thought had introduced himself as Twix—a sixtysomething black man in a military jacket with a thick gray beard—insisted that David take his camping chair near the fire. When David sat, one of the guys from the canopy kitchen thrust a hot bowl of stew stuffed with large chunks of carrots, potatoes, corn, and green beans into his hands. David thought it might have been the best vegetable stew he'd had in his life. It was certainly the first home-cooked meal he'd had in a while. He finished every last drop, and then they brought him another bowl without him even asking for it.

The teenager with the cornrows sat beside him. "You need anything, Mr. Shep?"

"No, I'm good, thanks. Larue, right?"

"Yessir."

"Cool name."

"Moms called me that when I was little. My real name is Lawrence."

"Where is your mom? If you don't mind my asking." David wondered how a teenager like Larue ended up living in the woods. Didn't seem right.

"She's dead. Got herself killed when I was eleven."

"I'm really sorry, Larue. What about your father?"

"Never knew my pops. See, Moms was a druggie and slept around to get high."

"I see. How long you been living out here?"

"Been out on the streets by myself since I was twelve. Been staying here at the Camp for about a year. Probably should be dead right now, if not for Benny. Before I got here, I'd been stabbed and left for dead. Would've probably bled to death if Benny hadn't found me and got me to the hospital."

"I'm glad he did."

"You like jazz, Shep?"

"Sure. You?"

"Oh, yessir! I been learning to play Art Tatum's 'Tiger Rag.' That dude could really play. Maybe the fastest fingers I done ever heard on the keys."

"You play piano, Larue?"

"I been learning. The boys bought me a keyboard. Benny says I got real talent. I wanna play over at Pete's. You know that place?"

"Pete's on Sixth?"

"Yessir. I'm gonna try out as soon as I got 'Tiger Rag' down."

"Cool. I'd love to come see you play."

Larue gave him a fist bump, then left to help with cleanup. For the next hour, David just sat by the campfire and took in the scene. Guys would come over to him here and there and ask him different questions about his life. They all acted like they really cared. He could hardly wrap his mind around it. Several of the men had tears streaming down their faces as they were singing. Other guys would walk over and wrap supportive arms around each other's shoulders. Men were serving each other hand and foot. He was sitting among twenty uniquely different men of all ages and creeds who were all living in some kind of utopic tent city in the middle of the woods. David felt like he'd walked into another world—a strange, homeless Narnia. He was mesmerized by it all. This was a far different scene from what he experienced every day at the law firm. There, men were only out for themselves—and David was chief among sinners. These guys didn't care a lick about where David was from, where he went to law school, or his class ranking. He doubted anyone would make a fuss that he'd slept for four months in a van as a kid because his family was so poor—they all slept in camping tents.

When it started to get late, the guys began drifting off to their tents. A few told David they had odd jobs to get to early in the morning. Others had to go out looking for part-time work. And since none of the guys had a vehicle, they all had to get up at the crack of dawn to catch different bus routes across town. Damn near every guy made one last pass by David to shake his hand again and offer a farewell.

"Time to go," Benny said, sidling up to David.

With his flashlight, Benny guided David back out the long trail toward his vehicle. They passed by Larue, who had replaced Curly as lookout. They exchanged another fist bump. Benny finally led David through the last set of trees and back into civilization. David spotted his Range Rover sitting at the curb. Fortunately, it looked like it still had all four tires.

"Who knows you're out here in the woods, Benny?"

"Not many. We like to keep it that way. Let's just say we're not paying rent to a landlord or anything like that. So don't go bringing all your lawyer buddies here tomorrow."

They shared a quick smile.

"I'll try to keep them away," David offered.

"We're real selective about who gets to visit the Camp."

"I can tell it's a special place."

"Indeed. I call it a village of dry bones."

David tilted his head. "Why?"

"You see, in the Scriptures, God led the prophet Ezekiel in a vision to the middle of a valley full of dry bones. He told Ezekiel to prophesy over the bones. 'Thus says the Lord God to these bones: Behold, I will cause breath to enter you, and you shall live.' In that moment, the bones started to come back to life and reattach, skin and flesh covered them, and new breath filled their lungs. This was prophecy for what God was going to do with his people, but the very same thing happens here at the Camp. Brothers enter this place all dried up, hopeless, and empty, but then the very breath of God refills their lungs." Benny put his hand on David's shoulder. "Most homeless are just dry bones, Shep, desperately wanting to come back to life."

David pondered the powerful imagery.

"Maybe we're all just dry bones, Benny."

"Indeed."

David turned to leave, but Benny stopped him by gripping his arm.

"Shep, one more thing, if you don't mind me saying. Stay off the pills. They're a quick path to darkness. Believe me, I know that firsthand."

David drew back, immediately felt defensive. How did Benny know about his blue pills? Had he left them out in his condo or in his vehicle? David was sure he hadn't. He was so careful not to be exposed. He was about to straight-up lie, call the old man crazy, but he just couldn't get himself to do it. Not tonight—not after everything he'd just experienced.

Instead, he told Benny, "I will."

FOURTEEN

A week later, David boarded a Gulfstream G550 that would fit up to six-teen passengers. Marty Lyons told David their client had purchased the private plane two years ago from ExxonMobil for $38 million. The seats were the best European leather. The plane had four flat-screen TVs on various walls; a full computer station with a printer, copier, and scanner onboard; and a plush leather sofa in the back that folded out into a full-size bed. Everything about the plane sparkled and shone appropriately. Thirty-eight million? David continued to be astonished at the level of luxury he was being introduced to in his first few months with Hunter & Kellerman. The Gulfstream was headed to New Orleans, where Lyons had scheduled lunch with their client, followed by a round of golf at an exclusive club. They'd be back home in Austin by late evening—every second of the day trip billed to their wealthy client.

Before leaving, David spotted a gray Ford Taurus pull up close to the plane. A man got out of the car, and Lyons greeted him. David leaned closer to the window. It looked like the same building security guy he'd encountered in the middle of the night in Nick's office several weeks back. What was he doing here? The black jacket was still in place, but the cap was gone, showing the guy had short white hair. David sud-denly flashed back to the man he'd seen in the shadows outside Nick's house that night. Could this possibly be the same guy? David watched as Lyons and the man huddled closely together for a few minutes and talked about something. Then the guy got back in his car, left, and Lyons finally joined David in the cabin of the plane.

"What did building security want?" David asked.

Lyons tilted his head. "Who?"

"The guy you were talking to out there. He's building security, right?"

"What? No, he's no one. He works for a client." Lyons quickly changed the subject to the plane. "What do you think of this beauty?"

David glanced back out the window. *Works for a client?*

"David?" Lyons repeated, snapping him back.

"Oh, yes, sir. The plane is incredible."

"Wait until we get in the air."

Moments later, the plane rocketed into the air and quickly settled in smooth skies.

"You enjoying yourself, David?" Lyons asked.

David sat in a spacious booth across from Lyons, who wore his usual $5,000 custom-made power suit. David knew the price of the partner's suits only because he'd spotted an invoice on Lyons's desk one day. David wore a dark-blue Calvin Klein number that had cost him a painful $1,500, a suit that Melissa had insisted he had to have in his closet *right now*. She'd already added a half dozen new suits and six pairs of dress shoes to his wardrobe over the past months. She was spending his new money at a feverish pace. David was beginning to wonder how much money it would take for him to ever feel comfortable in her world.

"Yes, sir," David replied. "Very much so. Thanks."

"Good. I want you to enjoy this treat. You've worked your ass off. This is just the beginning for you, so stick with me and keep it up."

Lyons had been using the phrase "stick with me" a lot with David over the past week—ever since he'd been moved next door to the partner.

After becoming Lyons's new guy, David had been tagging along with the partner damn near everywhere. Two nights ago, David had been sitting at a dinner table with Lyons and Senator Baskins. David could hardly believe it. Hell, only six months ago, he was still serving cheap beer to local college students while wearing a wrinkled T-shirt that was drenched in sweat. Now he was having dinner with a US senator. Life had changed a lot in a short amount of time. Earlier that week, he'd sat down in a hotel suite with a writer and a photographer from a popular local magazine for their upcoming "Austin's Hottest Bachelors" issue. There would apparently be a big social media voting campaign centered on the magazine article. Melissa was treating the whole thing like she was trying to get David elected to Congress. The week had been even more exhausting than usual for him since he'd made good so far on his promise to Benny to stay off the pills.

Across from him in the plane, Lyons was already getting tipsy. He'd downed several glasses of bourbon before they'd even lifted off. Lyons kept saying that David reminded him of himself thirty years ago. Lyons had also grown up with very little money. His father had been a cotton farmer who twice had lost his land before going completely bankrupt and turning to booze and women. His sweet old dad had put a bullet in his own head when Lyons was only twelve. Lyons had found him in the barn. Real nice. Lyons didn't let it hold him back. He went on to put himself through college by selling kitchen knives door-to-door. After graduating with honors from the University of Houston, Lyons got into Harvard Law School. And so on and so forth. David had already heard most of this spiel a few times—usually late at night in Lyons's office when the partner had already cracked open his wet bar.

Lyons insisted that the huge weights that had been placed on both of their shoulders during their difficult youths were good things. They gave them an edge over everyone else. With most new attorneys hired at H&K, Lyons had to somehow yank the silver spoons out of their asses before he could get any real work out of them. But not guys like David.

He and Lyons were cut from the same cloth. Hungry, determined, *and* absolutely ruthless. Lyons was so pleased that David was not afraid to stick the knife in deep and twist it. He insisted that quality was going to make David fabulously wealthy.

The partner's speech was already slurring—it was not yet ten in the morning.

David stared out the window. *Stick the knife in deep and twist it.* That was probably why David had no real friends at the firm right now, other than his mentor. Thomas was the only guy who still talked to him on a friendly basis—although most of what he got from Thomas lately were words of cautious warning. Thomas mentioned that he, too, had been Lyons's number-one guy many years ago. Until Thomas and Lori decided to have kids and *screwed up everything*. Thomas said that was a direct quote straight from the partner's mouth. Thomas said his father had a wise saying: *Be careful how close you dance with the devil.*

David reflected on those words as he gazed out the airplane window. He thought about what Nick had said just hours before hanging himself. *Lyons will take your soul.* His mind went back to the white-haired man whom his boss had just met with outside the plane. Who was that guy? He decided to probe a bit.

"Were you as shocked as everyone else about Nick?" David asked.

Lyons looked over, seemed to consider his words. "Frankly, no, I wasn't. I always felt Nick was a bit weak."

"Was he a good lawyer?"

"He was adequate. But that doesn't get the job done at places like Hunter and Kellerman."

David recalled Nick's other words. *You should get out before you run into real trouble—like me.*

"Nick ever cause you any trouble?"

"What's with all the questions?"

"Just trying to learn from the situation, that's all."

"You're not Nick, so don't worry about it. He wasn't built to handle the pressure of a big-money law firm like you and me. Unfortunately, it cost him his life. But let's not spend time kicking a man who's already in the grave, shall we?"

"Yes, sir."

David pondered his boss's choice of words. *It cost him his life?* Did he mean to say, it pushed Nick to take his own life? He stared back out the window, tried to set his mind on other matters. He thought about Benny and the boys in the Camp, as he often had over the past week. He hadn't seen Benny since that night in the woods. But he'd seen Larue, the teenager with the cornrows, out on the sidewalk of Congress Avenue yesterday. David was tagging along to a power lunch with Lyons and another partner when Larue suddenly stepped out in front of them. David connected eyes with the teenager, who clearly recognized him.

"Shep! Hey, man, it's me, Larue, from the Camp. How you doing, man?"

Lyons had given David a hard stare, clearly wondering why this black street kid in the dirty clothes was talking to their firm's new star like they were old friends or something. David had felt caught in the awkward crosshairs. It was too late to act like he didn't see Larue, as they were only a few feet apart; however, he buckled under the pressure of Lyons's intense glare and brushed right past Larue without saying a word to him.

When Larue had trailed them a little too close for comfort, still trying to get David's attention, Lyons had turned around and threatened the young man. "Go beg somewhere else, you punk, before I call the police on you."

As they kept walking, David took a glance back. Larue just stood there like a family member had slapped him across the face in public. David felt like the biggest ass on the planet and immediately regretted his choice. He'd driven over to East Austin last night, trying to find his way back to the Camp so he could apologize to Larue. But he only got turned around in the confusing streets. And there was no way to call Benny to get directions, since the man didn't own a phone. David hadn't slept well last night—the memory of the brutal exchange with Larue running so vividly through his mind all night. He really wanted to make amends.

"You ever saltwater-fish, David?"

David turned back to Lyons, who had a fresh glass of bourbon in front of him.

"No, sir."

"Eddie and I took this plane to Weipa, Australia, last summer. Best saltwater fishing on the planet. Fifty-five different species. Queenfish, barramundi, Spanish mackerel, you name it. That place was paradise. We're headed to Marbella, Spain, this fall. Supposed to have the biggest red tuna you'll ever see. And the best-looking babes. Hell, maybe we'll take you with us. What do you think about that?"

"Yes, sir, that'd be great."

"Then stick with me . . ."

FIFTEEN

They had lunch at Antoine's in the heart of the French Quarter with their client Eddie Ornen, the sixty-year-old CEO whose company owned the jet, along with Turk Rogers, one of Ornen's yes-man senior executives. Antoine's served up a feast of center-cut tenderloin of beef with fried potatoes, Béarnaise sauce with sautéed mushrooms, grilled trout with crawfish tails in white wine sauce, and fried soft-shell crabs. The three older men also quickly downed two bottles of expensive French wine, the names of which David couldn't pronounce.

Afterward, they all jumped into a black limousine and rode over to Timberlane Country Club for eighteen pristine holes of golf on what David was told was the first private golf club on the west bank of the Mississippi River. David noted that *nothing* about any litigation matter was ever discussed. It was pretty clear that Lyons and Ornen were simply fishing and golf buddies, and this was a good excuse for them to spend Ornen's company cash to jack around like old frat brothers. On the golf course, David played just well enough to not embarrass himself but not so well that he outclassed his boss—he was no dummy. There were several putts he'd missed to ensure that his boss beat him. Apparently, Lyons was no dummy, either, as he missed an easy four-footer on the eighteenth green to give his CEO buddy a one-shot victory on the day. They were then escorted over to the spa for massages and more drinking.

At that point, David asked Lyons if he could step out for a few hours. David said he had a family member nearby that he'd like to visit, if that was okay with his boss. Lyons was already drunk, so he happily excused David. But the partner warned David to have his ass back on the plane by ten o'clock, as they were racing down the runway with or without him.

David's older sister, Brandy Lee, lived on the outskirts of Denham Springs, a small town of ten thousand near Baton Rouge. Brandy's husband, Keith, coached eighth-grade football at Denham Springs Junior High. David had visited them only once before in Louisiana when their second son, Wyatt, was born. Wyatt was now three, and his older brother, Jackson, was five. Brandy had given up a low-paying teaching gig to stay at home and keep the two boys in line. His sister's family lived in a three-bedroom double-wide on a dull acre of country land near a dirty pond. Although it wasn't quite the dumpy RV trailer where they'd grown up, David considered it only a small step up. Brandy was still dirt-poor, with no real hope of ever climbing out.

Pulling the rental car to a stop in the dirt driveway, David immediately spotted the two small boys tackling each other in the front yard. Jackson had a football in his hands while Wyatt tried to rip it away from him. They went at it like brothers should. Both boys had shaggy brown hair and looked a lot like David did when he was their age. David noted sadly that Jackson was about the same age he was when his father had died. The two boys looked over at him when he got out of the car. Then David immediately heard the familiar squeal of his big sister coming from the front porch.

"David Marshall Adams! What are you doing here?"

Brandy came rushing off the porch and nearly tackled him to the ground, a huge hug that felt better than anything he'd experienced in a long time. He stumbled backward, trying to keep his balance, and squeezed her right back. Brandy had thick black hair, freckles on her cheeks, and the biggest blue eyes that always danced when she spoke to him. Although she'd put on a few extra pounds since he'd last seen her, she was still the spitting image of their mother. She looked beautiful. The two of them had been close growing up. When their mother had died before his last year of high school, David had quickly spiraled off the deep end. He was ready to quit football, quit school, and quit life. When he'd started to get into real trouble, Brandy dropped out of college, moved home, and basically pulled him by his hair kicking and screaming through a dark season. She'd all but saved his life.

"Hey, sis," David said, grinning.

Stepping back, Brandy examined him closely with both hands on his shoulders. "Let me look at you for a moment." She frowned. "You're not eating, Davey! I can tell. You look way too skinny. Don't they feed you at that high-falutin' law firm?"

"Yes, they feed us well, believe me."

She couldn't stop smiling at him. "Look at you in that fancy suit and all. Momma would be so proud of you. Such a big shot."

It was clear that living in Louisiana had done little to curb Brandy's thick West Texas twang; if anything, it was stronger than ever, her accent now tinged with a touch of the bayou. She sounded like the queen of Hicksville. But hearing her voice was like wrapping himself in a warm blanket. Damn, he missed her so much.

Turning to her kids, Brandy said, "Boys, get your little butts over here right now, and say hello to your uncle David. Don't be rude."

Wyatt and Jackson came over, both giving him awkward hugs because they clearly didn't know him too well. David had made little effort to be involved in their lives; he'd been so consumed by his own success. Brandy dismissed the boys, and they ran off again, trying to peg each other with the football the whole way.

"They've grown up, sis," David said.

"Yeah, well, they tend to do that. Those boys eat like horses, I tell you what." She turned back to David. "It's so good to see you. Why didn't you call first?"

"I wasn't sure I'd be able to make it out until now. I'm over in New Orleans meeting with a client today. I have only a brief window."

"I wish Keith was here. He's mowing at the ball fields right now. He has to do dang near everything himself these days. How long will you be able to stay?"

"Not long at all, I'm afraid. I have a plane to catch shortly."

"Well, all right. Then get over here and let me get you something to drink. I want to hear about every detail of your fancy new life."

They sat on the front porch in cheap lawn chairs. Brandy served him sweet tea from a plastic red cup. The two boys never stopped. They must've circled the double-wide twenty times already. Brandy said Wyatt was the future football star, like his uncle, which really made his older brother mad. Jackson was more of the bookish, creative type, like Brandy. He was learning to play the trumpet. They were good boys. Keith was doing well, too, Brandy mentioned. Her husband had a nice group of eighth graders this year. After two straight losing seasons, Keith thought they had a really good chance at a winning record. Her husband was also up for a promotion to the high school next year. The head varsity coach had told him he was all but a shoo-in to coach on the JV team. Brandy said they were praying really hard for it, because it would mean a $2,000 bump in his salary. They needed it really bad. The boys were getting so dang expensive. Jackson's trumpet had cost them over $100. Could David believe that?

Sitting there, David just smiled. He didn't have the heart to tell his sister that the tenderloin he'd just eaten in New Orleans had cost more than that. Or that his new suit cost about the same as Keith's potential bump in annual pay. He also knew better than to offer Brandy any of his new money—she'd be offended and throw it right back in his face. She was every bit as stubborn and prideful as their mother.

"Anyway, enough about me," Brandy said. "I want to hear all about your big-city life."

He shrugged. "Not much to tell, really, although it's definitely a little different from living around here."

"I certainly hope so!" she exclaimed. "You didn't study so hard at Stanford the past three years for nothing. So stop being modest. Tell me about the firm. Is working there everything you've always dreamed about?"

"And then some," he replied. "Hell, sis, I flew to New Orleans today on a thirty-eight-million-dollar private jet."

"Get out!" Brandy exclaimed, nearly flipping out of her lawn chair. "Are you serious?"

He laughed. "I'm serious. We just ate lunch at Antoine's in the French Quarter."

"I've seen that restaurant on TV."

"It's very good, believe me."

"What about girls?" Brandy asked, switching gears. "Do you finally have a sweet girl in your life?"

David pondered that question. *Sweet* was not exactly the word he'd use to describe the force that was Melissa Masters. "Yes, I'm seeing someone. Her name is Melissa."

"That's great! Tell me about her. Is she someone you'd want to bring to Denham Springs to meet your big sister?" She gave him a skeptical head tilt. "Or someone who'd be comfortable sitting next to me in a church pew, David Marshall?"

"Believe me, Melissa can hold her own in any environment. Although I probably won't be bringing her to Denham Springs any-time soon."

She frowned. "Fine, I won't push. For now. Are you having any fun in Austin? Do you have pics of your new condo? We only have an hour, David, so start spilling already!"

David gave her a few more details about the firm, how nice everything was in the offices, how he'd recently been celebrated in front of everyone by the partners and then moved into an even bigger office a few weeks ago. He was definitely on the fast track with the firm. He talked about the fancy dinners with senators, all the important functions he'd recently attended, and even his interview with a magazine for an upcoming profile. He shared pictures on his phone of his condo at the Austonian. He talked about the Range Rover. It was certainly easy to paint her a picture of a pretty glamorous life. Of course, he left out the part about the bottles of blue pills, how strung out he already felt, and how one of his colleagues had committed suicide recently because of job stress.

When he paused, Brandy didn't immediately insert herself again, like she'd been doing. This time, she just studied David with watchful eyes. He could tell something was brewing.

"What?" he asked her.

"You tell me."

"Tell you what?"

"Something's wrong, isn't it?" she asked.

"No. Why?"

Her eyes narrowed. "Don't lie to me, David. You know you could never lie to me and get away with it. So don't try to do it now. Okay?"

He sighed. "Give it a rest, Brandy."

"No, I won't! Tell me what's wrong."

David stared out toward the pond on the property. There was no use arguing with Brandy. She could be relentless in getting him to talk. She always used to force him to share his feelings when they were in grade school together, sometimes pinning him down on the floor of the trailer. She told him it wasn't healthy for him to bury everything on the inside.

He had to admit she was usually right.

"I don't know," he began, exhaling deeply. "What if you worked for something your whole life—I mean, you busted your ass for it and overcame all kinds of obstacles—only when you finally achieved it, when you *finally* got there, what if it's not what you really expected? What if it all starts to feel like some kind of big lie?"

"Someone lied to you at the law firm?"

He shook his head. "No, not exactly."

"I'm not sure I follow."

He swallowed. "It's more like I lied to myself, I think."

"Keep talking."

Standing, David walked over and leaned against a wooden railing on the porch. "I met this interesting group of guys recently. I mean, these were really great guys, Brandy. From the first moment I met them, they all treated me like I was family. The most genuine and happy-go-lucky guys I've ever been around. But these guys have absolutely nothing. I mean, *nothing*. No cars, no electricity, no working toilets, barely the clothes on their backs. Hell, they all live in camping tents in the middle of the woods. It's crazy. But honestly, most of them seem a whole hell of a lot happier than the guys I work with at the firm every day."

"Happier than you?"

"I didn't say that."

"Well, you don't have to have money to be happy."

"Yes, I know that."

"Do you really, David? Because I'm not sure I believe you."

"Come on, sis. Cut it out."

"Look, I'm just saying since middle school, nearly everything with you has always been about making money. You were always so dang embarrassed about us being so poor. You got into so many fights with the other boys when you felt like they were making fun of you for it.

You were always talking about making it all the way to the NFL, earning millions of dollars, so you could have a different life from what we had. You were *always* talking about buying big houses, fancy cars, and boats, when you *finally made it.*"

"Every young boy talks like that."

"True. But with you, it was somehow different. It was your singular obsession, especially after Momma died."

"Let's talk about something else, okay?"

Brandy wouldn't let it go. "Do you think I'm happy, David?"

"Of course I do."

"No, you don't!" she said, chastising him. "I saw it clear as day on your face the moment you stepped out of the car today. You can't fool me. *Poor Brandy, still living in a mobile home, still wearing worn-out old clothes bought at garage sales and barely able to even buy her son a stupid trumpet.* But you don't need to feel sorry for me. We're happy here. We don't have a fancy SUV, but we have more than enough. We have a good life. I wouldn't change it."

"Good for you."

She wasn't done with the lecture yet. "And you know what? Momma was happy, too."

David turned, frowned. "Stop it. Mom was miserable. We had *nothing.*"

"You're wrong. We had each other. And to Mom, that was enough."

"It *wasn't* enough, Brandy. Mom worked herself to death trying to give us more. She wouldn't be dead right now if she hadn't had to run to three different jobs her whole life, barely ever getting any sleep, just to put crappy cleats on my feet and somehow pay for all of my football camps."

"Mom is dead because it was her time."

"It wasn't her time!" David yelled, his face flush with anger. "Stop saying that!"

Brandy looked over at him with sad eyes, her voice softening. "Oh, Davey, I love you so much. You know that. But you've got to finally let Momma go already. It wasn't your fault. It wasn't my fault. It wasn't anyone's fault. I know you always wanted to take care of our mother. From the moment Dad passed, you were so determined to fill his shoes somehow, become the man of the house, and take care of our family. Momma and I used to call you the only six-year-old grown man we knew. You were such a chivalrous little boy, always wanting to help Momma out, never even letting her carry in the groceries herself. From early on, you made it your mission in life to grow up and take care of our mother. And now that you can finally do it, not getting the chance must hurt you a lot."

David looked away, his eyes growing moist. She was right.

"But Momma made her own choices, too," Brandy continued. "Did you know that when you were in the eighth grade and I was a sophomore, that Momma got offered a really good full-time job over in Midland? She'd met a nice lady at a church retreat there, they really hit it off, and the lady's husband owned a successful accounting firm. The pay would've been more than twice what Momma had been making. It was enough money that she probably could've finally moved us out of the trailer and into a real home. Maybe even get herself a car that didn't break down every other week. But she turned it down."

David looked over. "Why? That's crazy."

"She didn't want to move us. I had just joined the drill team and was finally making new friends after having trouble my freshman year. And Coach Taylor at the high school had already taken a real shine to you, even as an eighth grader, and he told Momma his big plans for you. You'd found a place to belong in that group of boys and began practicing even harder, if that was possible. Momma had started a Bible study with some sweet ladies that she really cared about and who were caring so well for her. She didn't want to move us away from all of that—even if it meant a lot more money. We were struggling but getting by at that point. No, we didn't have *anything* extra; that was for sure. And Momma would have to keep working multiple jobs to make ends meet. But she was okay with it. Momma knew that real happiness was found in relationships and not in nicer cars and bigger houses."

David felt a catch in his throat. "You never told me that before."

"I guess I was waiting for the right time."

SIXTEEN

The Gulfstream glided smoothly through the air on its way back to Austin. Lyons had been passed out drunk across from him nearly the entire flight—only waking up here and there to ramble on incoherently about something, or to stumble into the restroom to vomit. David found it embarrassing behavior for a man who led a successful litigation group for one of the most powerful law firms in Texas; a man who'd made over $4.5 million last year alone; a man who was regularly praised on the covers of national legal magazines; a man who'd been his idol and envy just a few weeks ago. At the moment, Marty Lyons seemed like nothing more than a rich fraternity punk.

Upon returning to the country club, David had inadvertently walked in on Lyons and Ornen engaged in some sketchy behavior with two young ladies outside the spa's steam room. Both men were married. Pretending not to notice, David had waited in the lobby for his boss to finally emerge. Later, Lyons had warned him in private that if David ever mentioned anything to his wife, he'd fire David on the spot—or have him killed. The second comment took him off guard. He thought Lyons was trying to be funny; however, it gave him pause. He couldn't shake the image of Lyons meeting with the same guy who had been outside Nick's house. The same guy who had been rummaging through Nick's office two days later. Who the hell was he? And what was he looking for? Lyons said he worked for a client. Which client? Could there possibly be something more behind Nick's suicide?

David felt a chill rush up his back. *Was* it a suicide?

Alert at the moment, Lyons's glassy eyes were on his cell phone in his fingers as he typed out a few things, probably trying drunkenly to reply to emails. Finished, he put his head back against the seat cushions and seemed to be out of it again. David glanced down at the man's phone that had fallen loosely onto his boss's chest. He had a sudden thought to snag the phone and peek at his messages—see if he spotted anything odd about Nick—but David knew he probably only had a few seconds to act before the phone locked with security. David felt a surge of adrenaline push through him. What if Lyons caught him?

Getting out of his seat, David leaned over his boss. Then he reached down and carefully plucked the phone from the man's chest, like he was playing the kids' Operation game and didn't want to get buzzed. Device in hand, David looked at the screen. The phone was still active and not yet locked. He felt his heart racing. He pressed an icon on the screen to keep it unlocked, and then he cautiously stepped around to the very back of the cabin.

He stared down at the screen, his fingers shaking. Where should he look first? He opened Lyons's email and did a search in the app for *Nick Carlson*, which brought up over five hundred emails between Nick and his boss over the past few years. Nick had worked on a lot of Lyons's cases. David thought about that. If Nick was just an adequate lawyer, why would his boss have him involved with so many of his clients?

David began scrolling, seeing if anything stood out to him as suspicious. But it all just looked like standard casework interaction. Most of the clients listed in the emails were familiar company names, but there were a couple he hadn't seen before. David made mental notes on those clients.

Lyons suddenly shifted in his seat, mumbled something. David stood perfectly still, not sure what he'd do if Lyons woke up and looked back in his direction. David would be crucified. His heart beating even faster, he quickly went back to the phone, switched gears, and began searching through text messages instead. Lyons was inundated daily with hundreds of texts. And it looked like his boss never deleted anything—which gave David some hope. He scrolled all the way back to the day Nick had committed suicide, just to see if he found anything.

He did.

The afternoon of his death, Nick and Lyons had exchanged texts.

Nick: We have to go to the police with this.

Lyons: We have a duty to protect our client. No police.

Nick: This isn't right. You know that.

Lyons: We've been over this already. Don't be a fool.

Nick: I think it's foolish to do nothing.

There was no return text from Lyons after the last one from Nick. And there was nothing above this particular text exchange that seemed to connect to this conversation. David wondered what this was all about. Police? What the hell?

His boss started talking out of nowhere, startling David.

"Eddie really liked you, David. Said you reminded him of his son."

Quickly shoving the phone in his pocket, David slipped into his seat across from Lyons again. The man had his eyes half-open. David prayed his boss wouldn't suddenly look down, realize his phone was missing, and start searching.

"I appreciate that," David replied. "Enjoyed golfing with him, for sure."

A sly grin appeared on Lyons's face. "Eddie cheats at golf. Always has. I saw him drop a new ball in perfect grass several times."

David didn't reply. He just stared at the man's eyes, hoping he'd go out cold again.

"You did good today, son," Lyons said. "Why don't you take some time for yourself tomorrow? Go roll around with Melissa. That's why I sent her. I know I would in your shoes."

David cocked his head. What did Lyons just say? David had never mentioned a word to his boss about dating Melissa. He thought back to the unexpected text from his boss that showed up on Melissa's phone while they were on their first date. She hadn't mentioned a word about Lyons over the past month. David had felt no real reason to push her on it—until now.

With his boss passed out again, David pulled Lyons's phone back out and searched for Melissa's contact info, which he easily found. Then he pressed a button to send her a text message and discovered a brief text strand between his girlfriend and his boss that began the first day he'd met Melissa.

Lyons: He'll be at Buffalo Billiards tonight around 11.

Melissa: Okay, I'll be there.

Five hours, twelve minutes later, another exchange.

Melissa: All is good. We're spending the day together on Sunday.

Lyons: Nice work.

Two days later, he found this time-stamped when they were having dinner at Eddie V's:

Lyons: Any update?

Then, an hour later:

Melissa: He doesn't seem too upset about Nick. But I think we're going to see each other again soon, so I'll probe a little more this week.

Lyons: Keep me posted.

Melissa: I will. But let's talk by phone from this point forward.

Lyons: Agreed.

That was the end of the texts.

David felt his stomach drop. He could hardly believe what he was reading. Lyons had set up his meeting Melissa? Why? Had she been lying to him about everything this past month? He remembered now that Melissa had asked early on about Nick's suicide and how David felt about all of it. He said he was fine and never went into any details with her.

What did she want to know?

More important, what did Lyons want to know?

SEVENTEEN

David drove straight from the airport to Melissa's house, where he banged on her front door until he woke her up. He saw lights pop on down the hallway, heard the poodle barking up a high-pitched storm on the other side of the door. Finally, Melissa answered wearing black silk pajamas with messy hair and a foggy look in her eyes.

"David?" she asked. "What's going on?"

"We need to talk right now," he demanded.

"Is everything okay?"

"No, it's not."

She let him inside the foyer. The poodle growled at him.

"Did something happen in New Orleans?" she asked.

He ignored her question. "Why were you at Buffalo Billiards the night we met?"

"What?"

"Please just answer my question."

"I told you already. I'd met clients there earlier that night."

"Which clients?"

"What's this all about? Why are you so upset?"

"I want the truth from you."

She stood there, mouth parted but not saying anything.

"I'm giving you an opportunity here, Melissa," David said. "I suggest you take it."

She dug in her heels, her eyes narrowing. "I don't like your tone."

"I don't like your lies."

"I'm not lying to you. So stop it!"

David knew right then and there it was over between them. He'd held on to some false hope that Melissa would immediately disclose the full truth and beg for forgiveness—and that might be enough to salvage something of their relationship. But that clearly wasn't happening. However, he still wanted to know the truth about her involvement with Lyons.

"How well do you know my boss, Melissa?"

She shrugged. "I told you. He's a client of our firm."

"That's it? He's just a client?"

"Yes. Why?"

"Do you ever have any direct interaction with him?"

"I mean, I see him here and there at different functions."

He almost laughed at her. "How long are you going to keep up this stupid charade? I know you've been corresponding with Lyons about me."

Melissa cursed, her shoulders dropping. "I didn't mean for it to go this far."

"So everything between us has been a lie?"

"No, I swear," she said. "It's not like that."

"Then tell me what it's like."

She sighed, swallowed. "Marty is one of my father's biggest clients. He said he had a sensitive client situation, and he was worried that you might reveal highly privileged attorney-client information because you were rattled about Nick Carlson's suicide. As a favor, he asked me to spend some time with you to see if anything came up about it. That's it."

"What privileged attorney-client information?"

"I don't know exactly. It all had to do with Nick Carlson."

David tried to put that together in his head. He hadn't worked on any client matters where Nick had been involved before his death. So it didn't make much sense to him.

"I wanted to tell you the truth, David," Melissa insisted.

"But you didn't. Not even when given a second chance tonight."

She frowned at him. "It's complicated, okay?"

"No, it's not. To me, it's simple. You chose to protect Daddy's money over building our relationship on trust. You showed your true colors."

Melissa didn't like being called a liar. So she turned on him. "Look, you can get off your high horse already. You're no Boy Scout, either, with your hidden bottles of pills."

David's mouth dropped open.

"That's right," Melissa added. "I've seen you secretly popping them when you think I'm not watching."

"I'm not taking them anymore."

"So what? You lied to me about them."

"I never lied. I just . . ." David didn't feel like arguing about who was the worse person between them and turning this into an even bigger drama. So he turned to walk out.

"Have a good life, Melissa."

EIGHTEEN

The next day, David drove over to a civic center on the east side where one of the city's nonprofits was hosting a homeless resource fair. He'd done some online searching, hoping to spot an opportunity where he might run into Larue and make amends. The resource fair had popped up on Google and seemed like as good a chance as any.

He got out of his car and walked over to the main building, where a long line of homeless folks had formed on the sidewalk. There was a band set up near the front of the building playing music and entertaining the ragtag group. Inside the main hall, David found a bustling crowd of both volunteers and those who were being served. There were signs at different stations all around the hall: HAIRCUTS, MEDICAL, IDs, JOB ASSISTANCE, LEGAL, and HOUSING. David noted that everything was orderly and civil. He wasn't sure what to expect, but all the guests were being very patient and considerate as they waited in the long lines. He did not immediately spot Larue or any of the boys he'd met at the Camp the other night. He went back outside.

In a side parking lot, several huge canopies had been set up with folding tables beneath them. Behind the canopies, he spotted volunteers stationed at portable grills, where they were rapidly producing cooked burger patties. A nice burger aroma hung in the air. Unfortunately, there was no sign of Larue anywhere outside, either.

"You here to help?" a short-haired lady asked him. Her name tag identified her as Ruth, the volunteer coordinator.

"Help how?" David asked.

"We're short in the food line. We could use you."

"Sure. Just tell me what to do."

She handed him a red apron from a box, said he'd be on burger duty. Tying on his red apron, David looked forward to passing out burgers. It felt good to do *something* where he couldn't directly bill a client or be rewarded financially. Plus, it took his mind off the whole confusing situation with Melissa and Lyons. David knew he couldn't bring up anything with his boss about it. That would only get him into trouble. But would Melissa report back that she'd been busted? Would that affect things for him around the office? Thankfully, David hadn't mentioned to Melissa how he'd discovered their secret arrangement in the first place.

David continued to search the faces but saw no sign of Larue anywhere. As a long line of homeless folks formed at the front of the burger station, David found his spot behind a table and met some of the other volunteers, who were just as happy to be there. He had a simple job—place burger patties on open buns and be extra friendly. He thought he could handle that. Suddenly, large containers of cooked patties were delivered to his table, and the food line was officially open for business.

David smiled, greeted, and quickly put burgers down onto the thick paper plates their guests carried with them. There were a lot of sincere thank-yous and *God bless yous* from those coming through the line.

David first noticed the woman in the red ball cap when she was kneeling next to an elderly black woman in a wheelchair carrying around several trash bags on her lap. The woman in the cap looked to be in her twenties, with a brown ponytail, a white T-shirt, tan shorts, and running shoes. She held a clipboard in her hands and seemed to be helping the elderly lady with something important. David was immediately drawn to her. And not just because of her looks—although she was very attractive in a tomboy kind of way. It was more the way she was interacting with the woman in the wheelchair. She hugged the lady, repeatedly patted her knee, and sat really close to her during their conversation. The brunette in the ball cap was not at all afraid to touch and engage with a homeless woman.

For the next hour, David worked up a good sweat serving burgers—more than a thousand of them, he guessed, as many of the guests returned through the food line two or three times until they were all stuffed. Ruth said that was just fine. Keep serving them. She instructed David to be generous and to *give, give, give*—both of the burgers and especially of himself. He liked Ruth a lot. She was passionate. Looking around, he realized he liked *everything* about this day.

As they began cleaning up, David again noticed the brunette in the red ball cap. She was standing by herself, jotting intently on her clipboard. He walked over to be closer to her. He noticed the tiny diamond stud pierced through her left nostril. There was a small butterfly tattoo on the back of her neck with a few words beneath it: *The greatest of these is love.* She seemed to notice his staring, looked up at him.

"Can I help you with something?" she asked.

She had the most engaging green eyes.

David shifted awkwardly. "You're really great with them."

She tilted her head, confused.

"Sorry, I've been watching you work," he clarified. "I was just saying you're really great with all of these people."

"You've been watching me?"

"Not in a creepy way, I swear."

She gave a curt smile. "Your first time serving *these people*?"

He realized he'd stupidly made an unnecessary distinction between himself and the guests. "Sorry, I promise you I didn't mean anything by that."

"Don't worry about it."

He stepped closer, held out a hand. "David Adams."

She shook it firmly. "Jen Cantwell."

"Do you work for one of the nonprofits?"

"I run the *Advocate*. A newspaper that serves the homeless."

"Really? I'll have to get a subscription."

Another small smile. "You really are clueless, aren't you?"

"Oh, I'm guessing I can't have the *Advocate* delivered to my condo?"

"No, you can't. Our street friends sell the newspaper on corners around the city to try to put a little money in their pockets and better serve their own community."

"That's cool. I like the way our street friends try to take care of each other. I don't see that too much in my world. It was the same when I was out at the Camp the other day. All the guys were really looking after each other."

"What camp?" she asked him.

David shrugged. "I don't know. They all just called it *the Camp*."

"Who called it that?"

"Guys named Benny, Doc, Shifty . . . Do you know any of them?"

"You've been to Benny's camp?"

David nodded. "I'm not really supposed to talk about it."

"Why were you at their camp?" Jen asked. "Didn't you just tell me today's the first time you've even served the homeless?"

"It's a crazy story, actually."

NINETEEN

Jen Cantwell wanted to hear all about David's crazy story. She admitted she was intrigued as to why someone like David Adams—a clear fish out of water—had been invited to visit a place as secretive as the Camp. Because she had to leave the resource fair early on Saturday, she asked if David would be willing to meet her the following morning at seven on the running trails by the First Street Bridge. David found it an odd time and location to meet—after all, it was Sunday, with the sun barely up. Nevertheless, it worked well for him, as he could still be at the office early enough for a full day of billing. Lyons had given him some grace yesterday, but he knew not to push it too far.

He arrived a few minutes early and was surprised to find a big crowd already gathering—probably around a hundred people. Something was clearly going on here this morning. A majority of the crowd looked like the group he'd served burgers to the day before. They were all huddled near a tree by the banks of Lady Bird Lake, with the downtown landscape just on the other side of the river.

Jen was already there. David found her just as he had the previous day, wearing blue jeans and a white cotton pullover and hugging a woman wearing rags with frizzy gray hair.

"You actually came," she said, as David walked up to her.

"Was there ever any doubt?"

"You'd be surprised how fast the euphoria of serving those in need can wear off with most people. It usually happens overnight."

"Not to me. Coffee?" he asked, holding up a carton containing four different cups that he'd picked up at Caffé Medici on his walk over from the Austonian. "I wasn't sure what kind of coffee you liked, so I just brought an assortment with me."

She smiled at him. He noted the cute freckles on her cheeks. The diamond nose stud was still in place. She wore very little makeup and didn't need a drop of it.

"I actually don't drink coffee," Jen admitted.

"Oops."

She laughed. "But plenty of people here would love the treat."

Jen took the tray and quickly gave the coffee away to four of her nearby homeless friends, who all gratefully accepted, no matter the make or flavor. David wished he'd brought a dozen more cups with him.

"What's going on here, Jen?" David asked, the crowd growing.

"It's an annual memorial service for all the friends we've lost on the streets during this past year." She pointed over to the large oak tree close to the water, which seemed to be the focal point of the gathering. "We call that the Tree of Remembrance. It was planted there more than twenty years ago at the very first memorial service. Come on, they're about to get started."

They navigated to the front of the crowd and closer to the tree. A man behind a microphone called everyone together. Jen whispered that he was an author who'd written several books on homelessness. The speaker took a few minutes to offer some stark realities about life on the streets. He said that although those on the streets were invisible to most, they were not invisible to everyone, hence the nice crowd this morning. He then went on to read a passage from one of his books. As he did, David took a moment to scan the crowd, again hoping to spot Larue. There was no sign of the kid, but he did notice Benny and some of the other boys from the Camp standing across the way from him. All of them looked very somber. David wondered how many friends Benny had lost in the past year. Did a lot of people die while living out on the streets of Austin?

A city councilman took the microphone next. He talked about properly mourning the deaths of friends but to not let it steal away hope. Hope for change. Hope for the value of human life. Hope for equal justice. He praised the efforts of so many of the nonprofits in the city who were doing so much to make days like today less devastating. When he finished, a folk singer came up with a guitar and sang a song that echoed that same hope.

Another man walked up to the microphone and said it was time to read the list of those they were all there to mourn from the past year—may they rest in eternal peace. He began to slowly read names off a list. As he did, people from the crowd began walking forward, some with flowers to place at the tree's base, others with handmade origami swans that they hung from various tree branches. There were many tears because there were *a lot* of swans hanging from the tree by the time the reader was done. Probably more than a hundred names had been read. David was stunned. How could that many people have died on the streets of Austin without him ever hearing *anything* about it? The folk singer did one more song, this one a bit happier. Finally, a local minister offered a closing prayer, the service concluded, and the crowd slowly began to disperse.

"How many did you personally know, Jen?" David asked.

"Dozens."

"Damn. I'm really sorry."

As the crowd shifted away, Benny and the boys from the Camp came over to see David, each of the men greeting him with the same warm embrace they'd offered him the other night. After giving Benny a hug, David said hello to Doc, the tall beanpole of a man; Elvis, with the sideburns; and Curly, with the thick mop of hair. Jen seemed to know the boys, too, including Benny, as they exchanged some pleasantries. At David's request, Jen took a picture on his phone of Benny and him standing together, arms over each other's shoulders.

"Benny, do you know where I can find Larue?" David asked.

"He's here and there. Kid stays busy. Why?"

"I really need to talk to him."

David wondered if Larue had said anything to Benny. By the blank look on the old man's face, David guessed the kid hadn't told him about their awkward interaction on the sidewalk.

"He's been over at the library a lot lately."

"Okay, I'll try there. Thanks."

When Benny and the boys had left, Jen's eyes narrowed in on David. "Okay, I've got to hear this story already."

They had breakfast at the Magnolia Cafe. David told Jen about his first encounter with Benny that dangerous night in the alley when the old man had likely saved his life. And then the subsequent trip to his condo. Jen had a good laugh at the image of David dragging Benny through the lobby of the glitzy Austonian. Then David told her about getting invited out to the Camp. Although Jen had heard about the place, she wanted to know *everything*. David gladly shared the details with her. It was fun watching her big eyes light up with each new revelation.

Concluding, David said, "It was truly unlike anything I've experienced in my life."

Jen couldn't stop smiling. "I still can't believe you got invited. They are *very* protective of their camps. The police are constantly trying to bust them up because they are usually camping on someone's private property. Or the neighbors are complaining about property values with the riffraff nearby. A lot of these camps can be vestibules for drugs. But I'd heard this place was really special."

"You heard right," David said, scooping up a bite of waffle.

"The guys seem to really like you, too," Jen added.

"Why're you so surprised? I'm actually a likable guy."

Jen grinned. "Why do they all call you Shep?"

David laughed, shook his head, and explained his first conversation with Benny. "After that, Benny just started calling me Shep. I guess I'm stuck with it." He shrugged. "I've been called a lot worse the past few months."

"Was it because of your experience with the Camp that you decided to show up at the resource fair yesterday?"

"Sort of." He didn't really want to tell Jen how he'd treated Larue the other day. Not when it seemed like she was warming up to him. "I think I'm having a midlife crisis."

"Right. You're what? Twenty-five years old?"

"Yeah, but I feel like I'm already fifty."

"They're working you that hard over at Hunter and Kellerman?"

His eyes narrowed. He hadn't told her that yet. "Wait, how'd you know I work at Hunter and Kellerman? Did you already Google me?"

She seemed a tad embarrassed. "I had to make sure I wasn't meeting up with a psychopath, that's all."

He grinned. "What about you? Why'd you leave a high-profile newspaper gig in DC to come work here for the *Advocate*?"

It was Jen's turn to act surprised.

He shrugged, smiled. "I also had to make sure I wasn't meeting up with a psychopath."

She playfully tossed a small piece of biscuit at him but went on to tell David her story. After graduating with honors from Columbia Journalism School, she got offered an entry-level reporter job at the *Washington Post*. Her dream job. She shadowed one of the big-deal investigative reporters on staff and worked her ass off. Then her brother, Jack, who'd been in the army, came home from a tour in Afghanistan, where he'd experienced some difficult things. Although Jack wouldn't talk much about it, Jen knew through her military contacts that he'd had several buddies die right next to him during an explosion. A couple of survivors had lost arms and legs. When Jack returned to the States, he suffered from severe PTSD. He had trouble acclimating to normal life. He couldn't keep a steady job and quickly spiraled into serious depression. Unbeknownst to the family, Jack started using drugs, so things got a lot worse for him. One night, he snapped and became violent with their mother, so their father kicked him out of the house. Told him to get cleaned up and not to come back until he did. They didn't hear anything from Jack for over nine months.

"Then I get an email out of the blue from my brother," Jen said. "He said he was living on the streets of Austin and needed my help. He said I was the only person he would ask. Our dad would never understand or even care. Could I come get him?"

"What'd you do?"

"I emailed him right back and said yes, of course. But I never got a reply. So I jumped on a plane and came to Austin to look for him. A couple of days of searching the streets and shelters turned into over three weeks. I couldn't find my brother anywhere. Several people on the streets thought they recognized his picture, but no one had a clue where he was. I was so desperate. The *Post* needed me back in DC, but I couldn't possibly leave town without finding my brother first. Then I got the call. Someone had found my brother. Jack was dead. They found him alone in the woods, camping all by himself. He'd overdosed."

"Jen, I'm so sorry."

"I visited his campsite. I had to see where my brother took his last breath. He died all alone inside a box tent in the middle of nowhere. I was devastated. One of the only things on him was a picture of the two of us riding our bikes together as kids. I cried something fierce out there in the woods. I wanted to be there for him, but I was too late. Although I tried to go back to my normal life in DC, I just couldn't shake it. My heart was still in Austin. So I finally quit my job, packed my bags, and moved to Texas two years ago, determined to somehow make a difference. I'd met a lot of good people who were doing meaningful work during my month searching for my brother. One of them owned the *Advocate*, so here I am."

"You're making a difference. I can tell."

She shrugged, fiddled with her spoon in her bowl of oatmeal. "Some days I do feel that way. But days like today, when you hear that many names read off a list, remind me that there is still so much work to be done. Several of the names on that list were young men just like my brother. I like the work I'm doing. Putting together the *Advocate* every month feels meaningful. It helps put money in their pockets. But it never feels like enough."

After a moment of quiet consideration, David decided to be vulnerable. "We were homeless for four months when I was a kid."

Jen looked up at him, surprised.

He continued. "My mom, my sister, and I lived in a broken-down van in the parking lot behind a church because we'd been kicked out of our trailer. We were really poor, Jen. My dad died in a car crash when I was only six, and we had no other family support. My mom did the best she could, working up to three jobs at a time, but we just barely held it together most of the time. I've thought a lot about those days in the past week, ever since visiting the Camp. I was close to becoming one of the young guys I met out there. When my mom died suddenly before my senior year, I tried to quit everything and just run away. Flip the bird to this cruel world and everyone in it. I started drinking heavily, looking for other drug escapes, and acting out in really destructive ways. I even stole a car one night, just for the hell of it. I was in pretty bad shape and didn't care anymore."

"How'd you come out of it?" Jen asked.

"Brandy, my sister. She moved back home from college and started kicking my butt around, the way I always needed from her. By sheer force of her will, she got me back on the right path. Everything I have today is because of her."

"God bless her. The single greatest cause of homelessness is the profound, catastrophic loss of family. Unfortunately, a lot of the guys at the Camp didn't have a big-sister safety net."

Sitting there, David realized he'd never told *anyone* that part of his story. Not his college buddies at ACU, not his classmates at Stanford. Not professors. Not the few girlfriends he'd had during college. Not Melissa. Certainly no one at the firm. He never wanted anyone to know about that part of his past—he thought it made him look weak. And he couldn't afford to ever look weak in his world. David wondered why he'd so easily told Jen.

"Is that why you wanted to become a lawyer?" Jen asked.

He shrugged. "I knew lawyers made a lot of money if they worked really hard. So after I got hurt playing ball freshman year, I set my sights on law school. I rolled up my sleeves and worked twice as hard as anyone else around me. That got me into Stanford. I kicked ass while I was there, and I got several high-paying job offers. I took the one at Hunter and Kellerman. I swore a long time ago I would do whatever it took to never be poor like that again."

"Seems all of your hard work has paid off."

"I suppose."

Her eyes narrowed. "Why do you not sound overly happy about it?"

"I am. It's just . . . nothing." He was starting to feel a little *too* exposed, so he quickly changed the subject. "Tell me more about how the *Advocate* works."

TWENTY

David found Nick's girlfriend, Carla, on Facebook and then reached out to her through email. She agreed to meet him on Sunday night at Dell Children's Medical Center, where she was an ICU nurse. They sat on a bench in a well-landscaped courtyard surrounded by the serenity of several water fountains. A short brunette in scrubs, Carla looked exhausted. She told him she'd just finished a difficult twelve-hour shift.

"I appreciate you meeting with me," David offered.

"You worked with Nick at the firm?"

"Yes, well, sort of. I'd just started when, you know . . ."

"That place is a real sweatshop. Nick and I barely saw each other."

"How long had you two been dating?"

"About six months."

"So you were serious?"

"About as serious as two people could be who both put in long hours."

"It must have come as a shock to you."

She nodded. "I still can't believe it. Every morning when I wake up, for just a moment, I hope it was all a bad dream. I mean, Nick was stressed out all the time because of his work, but I would've never expected this. It still doesn't make any sense to me. We had just talked about marriage two days before . . ." She bit her bottom lip, her eyes growing moist.

"I'm really sorry, Carla."

She sighed. "I've been picking up double shifts here at the hospital, just so I don't have to think about it all the time. My counselor says I'm delaying dealing with it, but I don't know what else to do. I'm so sad but so angry with him at the same time."

"Did Nick tell you what was stressing him out so much?"

"All of it. The hours, the cases, the pressure. No offense, but I'd already grown to hate your firm before this happened."

"I understand. Did he say anything specific about his work?"

She thought about it. "There was always something going on over there that had him worked up. His boss could be *really* hard on him."

"Believe me, I know. Nick and I talked about it. Did he ever mention wanting to go to the police about something related to a client?"

She looked up, like something registered. "Yeah, he did, actually. The day before, he'd mentioned he'd gotten an email from someone who was trying to blackmail one of his clients."

"Really? He say what it was about?"

"No. We were on the way out the door and in a hurry."

"He say which client?"

She shook her head. "No, he didn't like to talk about work too much when we were together. Neither did I. Which is why I think we were so good together." She looked over to David. "Why're you asking me all these questions?"

David wanted to be careful not to say anything that would upset Carla further. Especially when he really didn't know what he was searching for just yet.

"I'm just trying to understand," David said. "That's all."

"I'm not sure I'll ever be able to make sense of what Nick did."

TWENTY-ONE

David met Thomas for an early breakfast at a café a block from their office. David devoured French toast covered in powdered sugar, butter, and syrup. Thomas ate the garden omelet and strongly encouraged David to start guarding his health better if he didn't want to have a heart attack by forty. David figured he was in for another stern lecture of some sort, which was fine. At least someone at the firm actually cared about him in a way that was not directly related to his overall billing sheets.

Staring out the front window, David had noticed an old man with a shaggy beard and a dirty camouflage jacket sitting on the sidewalk. He looked a little like Benny. They were probably around the same age. The man held a cardboard sign in his lap that read: ARMY VETERAN. ALL HELP IS APPRECIATED. GOD BLESS. The man didn't say much—he just sat there on the sidewalk, staring off into space. David noted that, in the ten minutes he'd been sitting inside the café, not a single passerby had uttered a word to the man, or dropped anything into the man's Styrofoam cup. They all just scooted around him as if he were a pothole to be avoided. David wondered how often he'd done the same thing over the years.

"How was New Orleans?" Thomas asked, sipping on his orange juice.

David shook his head. "Interesting, I suppose." He quickly filled Thomas in on the Gulfstream, lunch at Antoine's, the golf, and finally their boss's drunken and despicable behavior with a young woman while inside the spa. He left out the part about breaking into Lyons's phone while on the plane ride back and discovering the text exchange with Nick. David still wasn't sure how to navigate this situation. A big part of him just wanted to cast it all aside and get on with his new life as a rich attorney. But then the image of Nick hanging by his neck kept showing up in his dreams and turning them into nightmares.

"Pretty common knowledge around the firm, I'm afraid," Thomas explained. "Lyons does what he wants, when he wants, both at work and at home. I've even seen it happen at firm parties with Sharon in the same room. I think she puts up with it because she likes the big house on the lake, the one in the mountains, the ranch, and the monthlong shopping trips in Europe. She's not the only partner's wife who puts up with more than they should. I tell you what, Lori would kick my ass sideways if she ever found out I was even *talking* inappropriately with another woman. And Lori would know, I promise you. I can hide *nothing* from her."

David grinned. "Well, at least I got to see my sister and nephews, so all was not lost on the trip. Lyons says he wants to take me saltwater fishing in Spain."

"Keep setting billing records, I'm sure you'll get to travel all over the world."

"You act like that's a bad thing."

"No, it's not all bad. I've just been around here long enough to see this pattern repeated. Every few years, a new guy will catch Lyons's eye, and he'll start tossing around the word *protégé* in the hallways. Honestly, David, it's probably the worst place you can be. The other associates quickly grow to hate you. And you work yourself into the ground trying to live up to Lyons's unrealistic expectations. It's a no-win situation. One day, I hope you'll wake up and realize this is a long game, not a short one. The problem with you rookies is that there's glory in the sprint. And glory can be like crack at places like Hunter and Kellerman."

"So who was the protégé before me? Let me guess. Hoskins from Northwestern?"

Thomas shook his head. "No, it wasn't Hoskins, although he's a good lawyer. It was a guy named Derrick Moore. Graduated number one from Duke. A good kid. You remind me of him in a lot of ways. Really smart and lots of energy. He hit the ground running. Not quite at your pace, but he was going at it hard. Of course, that made Lyons warm up to him real quick. He peppered Derrick with praise and moved him in next door. Soon came the bonuses and the exotic trips, along with the hollow look in Derrick's eyes."

"So what happened to him?" David asked, brow bunched. There was no Derrick Moore still with the firm. "He get recruited away to another big shop?"

"The opposite, actually. Derrick got hooked on cocaine and lost control. He crashed and burned in spectacular fashion. It happened at the firm's Christmas party, of all places. Derrick arrived stoned out of his mind, wielding a revolver, and telling everyone at the party he was going to shoot Santa Claus. It was total chaos before security quickly came and got him. We later found out there were at least no bullets in the gun. Needless to say, Derrick didn't last long afterward. The firm got him into a rehab clinic and then basically cut all ties to him. Last I'd heard, Derrick had relapsed again and lost his law license altogether."

"Damn," David muttered, thinking about the blue pills.

Thomas took another bite of his vegetarian omelet. "I keep telling you, the firm can make you do stupid things. You can easily lose yourself if you're not careful. The relentless chase, the hours, the power grabs, the politics, and of course, the money. Hell, it's better than crack. Until the money becomes your prison cell."

"How do you mean?"

"I see it all the time," Thomas declared. "If we're not wise to it, we can quickly build ourselves a prison of affluence. The best houses, the best cars, the best vacations. If we have kids, which many of us do, we send them to the best private schools, clubs, and summer camps. We max out our lives at every turn. Early on, we don't think too much about it, because we know as long as we stay in the game and keep grinding, the money will continue to grow. So we spend away. Our wives get used to spending away. We want them to be happy, because we're never at home, so we encourage them to enjoy the money. Even our kids get really comfortable with it, as they have the best video game systems and sports gear. Of course, the partners encourage us to overindulge, because they know the truth—if we do it, they'll own us. Before we realize it, we take a hard look around us and feel trapped. We feel like we can never break free without disappointing damn near every person in our lives."

David considered that line of thought. "Lyons actually encouraged me to *not* get married or have any kids until I made partner, if then. He suggested it was a surefire way to kill my drive and hook detrimental anchors around my own feet."

"A real romantic, that Marty Lyons."

David studied Thomas a moment. "If everything you're saying is true, Thomas, then why the hell do you stay? Or have you already built your own prison cell?"

Thomas's lips slowly curled up at both ends, as if he were giddy about what he was going to share with David next. "On the contrary, my man. I'm about to make my prison break."

David eyeballed him. "What do you mean?"

"It's why I wanted to have breakfast with you outside the office today, so I could tell you face-to-face. I'm turning in my resignation to Lyons this afternoon."

David's mouth dropped open. "You can't be serious?"

Thomas never flinched, the lines in his face firm. "I'm as serious as the heart attack you're going to have if you keep eating like a teenager."

"Wait . . . are you joining another firm?"

His mentor smiled wide again. "Not even close."

"Then I don't get it. What the hell are you going to do?"

"I'm starting my own firm."

David dropped his fork on his plate. "I don't believe you. You're probably only two years away from making partner. Your income will nearly triple."

Thomas shook his head. "Damn, QB, have you not been listening to me? Making partner cannot be your end goal. Have you noticed any of the partners actually working any less than us? Hell no! If anything, they all dive even deeper into the madness of that machine. You don't get your freedom when you finally make partner there—you officially terminate all rights to the rest of your life."

David cursed, drawing attention from nearby tables. "Sorry, I'm just surprised by this news."

"I can see that."

"I mean, I'll admit I've overheard other associates talking about it. Mostly the guys who've already been in the grinder for several years, like you. The topic of walking away seems to be a common fantasy talked about over beers. But no one ever actually does it. No one *ever* walks away. The money is just too damn good."

"Well, call me Columbus, because I'm setting new sails. Look, I'm not planning on being broke, okay? I can still make decent money on my own. But I can do much more meaningful legal work in the process. Sure, I'm probably not going to be jumping on any Gulfstream, or saltwater fishing in Spain, but I'll for damn sure be at every single one of my girls' soccer matches and dance recitals over the next decade. And I'll no longer have to worry about an irrational, half-drunk lunatic barking in my ear on my cell phone—literally cursing me out and demanding that I immediately get my ass back to the office—right smack in the middle of one of my girls' birthday parties."

David cocked his head at the mention of that.

"True story," Thomas confirmed.

"Sheesh." David exhaled, cursed again. This time more quietly. He still couldn't believe Thomas was actually doing this. "What kind of law will you practice?"

"Mainly family law. Children's issues. I'd like to do some work with the foster care system. Help with adoption matters. I'll still handle litigation matters for smaller companies who can't afford the big boys, like H and K, but I want most of my work to mean something more. I've already found a space on the second floor of the James H. Robertson Building. It's not much—just three little offices. It won't have ten-thousand-dollar rugs in the lobby, but it'll do the trick. I'm signing the lease today."

"That building is directly across the street from H and K."

"Correct. Right next to the Speakeasy."

The Speakeasy was a three-level bar with 1920s-style decor.

"Unbelievable. What do you think Lyons is going to say?"

"Doesn't matter. He can kiss my ass. I'll probably say that to his face."

David smiled at that thought. What he wouldn't give to be in Lyons's office to see that exchange. "Speaking of Lyons, let me ask you something. Have you ever known him to do something *really* bad when it comes to handling one of his clients?"

"You mean unethical?" Thomas queried.

"I mean . . . criminal."

"No. The man certainly pushes the ethical line around to get the results he wants, but I haven't seen him overtly break the law."

"Have you ever seen a guy in the office who works with one of Lyons's clients who has a buzz cut of short white hair, probably late thirties?"

"Not that I recall. What's with the questions?"

David considered telling Thomas his concerns but then decided against it. His mentor was walking out of H&K today as a free man, and David didn't want to spoil the moment for him.

"Nothing, man," David replied. "Are you *sure* you want to do this? If you leave and it doesn't work, you can't come back. Lyons would never allow it."

"Lori and I have been considering it for two years now. We've been saving up to make the leap. It's time."

David's initial shock was slowly wearing off. "Foster care? Adoption? I'm going to have to start calling you Saint Thomas."

"I'd rather you call me partner."

David cocked his head. "What?"

"I want you to join me, David."

David's mouth dropped wide open again. "You mean, like Gray and Adams, Attorneys at Law?"

Thomas shrugged. "Or Adams and Gray, I don't care. I have no ego with this."

David's head was again reeling. "I don't . . . I don't even know what to say. I think you've been drinking too many cocktails at the Speakeasy. I just got started at H and K."

"Yeah, I realize that," Thomas agreed. "But you're better than that place, and I can't say that about most of the other associates. I don't think most of those guys have much left of their souls. But you're a good lawyer who actually cares about real people. You sometimes act like you don't care, because that's the culture around there, but I can tell otherwise. I just don't want to see that place change you, that's all."

David struggled with a response. The thought of walking away from H&K was nowhere on his radar. But Thomas had been so good to him the past month, so he tried to play along for a moment. "Okay, hypothetically speaking, what kind of salary are we even talking about?"

"No salary," Thomas admitted. "We'd be full-on partners and evenly split all profits. I've saved enough to give us a year to make a strong go at it."

David leaned back, ran his fingers through his hair. "A year? This is crazy, man."

"Crazy enough to work. And think of all the benefits."

"What benefits?"

"Your commute wouldn't change."

"If I were to go with you, I couldn't afford my condo. I couldn't afford much of anything. I'd probably be sleeping on your couch."

"No, you could have one of my girls' bedrooms."

"What about health insurance? Would we even have it?"

Thomas laughed. "Okay, not really sure about that just yet. But how about Hawaiian shorts and flip-flops on Fridays?"

David didn't laugh. "With all due respect, Thomas, if you think I'm going to join you on this deal, you've lost your mind."

"I think I've *finally* found it," he countered, turning serious again. "Look, don't answer me on this right away. I understand this is all a bit of a shock this morning. I just want you to think about it for a while. Hell, take a few months; the offer will remain out there. If and when the time is finally right for you, you'll know, trust me."

TWENTY-TWO

David got a surprise call around eleven that night. Per usual, he was still at his office desk. The H&K hallways were quiet. Even Tidmore had already gone home. His rival had seemed defeated of late and was no longer seriously challenging David about who was going to leave the office first each night. The phone call was from Benny, of all people. He said he was inside the lobby of his building—could he come up to see him? David called down to building security and asked them to allow the old man up the elevator.

David met Benny in the firm's lobby. "You okay?"

Benny nodded, seemed just fine. He wore his usual trench coat, black knit cap, and work boots, although he was carrying a small black duffel bag with him. "Yes, I'm fine. Sorry to just show up at your office like this, Shep, but I was downtown tonight handling another matter. I thought you might still be working based off what you've told me about this place. You sure it's okay for me to be here? I don't want to get you in trouble."

"Of course!" David replied, although he knew it was only okay because no one else was in the office tonight. That thought was discouraging. Benny would probably never make it past the receptionist—she'd have security up there so fast, it would make Benny's head spin.

Although he hated to admit it, David was glad the old man hadn't come knocking during normal work hours and put him in the same awkward position that Larue had on the sidewalk the other day. He still had not had the opportunity to tell the kid he was sorry.

"Let's go back to my office, Benny."

He led Benny down the pristine hallways. The old man seemed to be taking in everything, his eyes bouncing from office to office. When they got to his office, David cleared a stack of binders from one of his leather guest chairs and invited Benny to make himself comfortable. As the old man sat and placed his duffel bag on the carpet by the chair, Benny seemed a tad uneasy. David wondered if he was uncomfortable being at the firm. He didn't figure the old man had been inside too many high-dollar offices like this one over the past ten years. Or maybe ever.

Sitting in his chair, David said, "So what brings you downtown this late?"

"My friend Willy. He's been having health issues. I think he might have pneumonia, so I dragged him over to Saint David's a few hours ago. Willy is so stubborn. If not for me, he'd probably lay there in the park all night, hacking up a lung, until he damn near coughed himself to death."

"You're a good man," David said.

"We've got to look after each other out there."

"I agree. You want something to eat? We still have leftover Chinese food in the kitchen from a catered dinner earlier tonight. I could warm you up a plate, if you want. It'd be no trouble at all. What do you say?"

"If it's no trouble, that'd be real nice of you, thanks."

"Sure thing!" David hopped up, welcoming an opportunity to show Benny some hospitality. "You just sit here and relax, okay? Make yourself at home. If you want, you can even finish up that legal brief sitting there on my desk."

David winked at Benny, who laughed.

"I haven't gone back to law school just yet, Shep," Benny said.

Leaving his office, David crisscrossed the quiet hallways until he entered the firm's spacious kitchen. There were two circular tables in a corner surrounded by chairs. A flat-screen TV on the wall showed a local news station. He stepped over to the two stainless-steel refrigerators, which were always stuffed full of extra food, so no associate ever felt the need to venture outside the walls of the firm. Opening the first one, David found several large plastic containers of Chinese food. From a cabinet, he grabbed a plate and began loading it to the edges with chicken fried rice, shrimp chow mein, sweet and sour pork, and sesame chicken.

Placing the plate in the microwave, he warmed it up for a few minutes. While he was waiting, he turned back to the TV and casually watched. The news station cut away to a series of local commercials. The first was a car dealer wearing a leotard who was engaged in an outlandish wrestling match with a muscle-bound guy. The car dealer was talking about putting a headlock on car prices, or something really dumb like that. David did a quick double take at the TV screen. There was something familiar about the other guy in the commercial. When the microwave dinged, David grabbed the plate, snagged a cold bottle of water from the fridge, and headed back to his office.

Returning, he found Benny standing inside Marty Lyons's corner office next door. The office lights were on, and Benny was staring over toward the expansive windows that looked out over the vast city. "That's one incredible view, Shep."

"Yeah, the best view on the entire floor," David agreed, before quickly ushering Benny out. He didn't think Lyons would be too happy to know that a homeless man had been in his office tonight. David didn't need another reason to have Lyons yell at him.

Returning to his office, David handed Benny the plate of food and the water bottle.

"Man, Shep, this looks good. Thank you."

Benny sat in the guest chair again while David returned to his executive chair.

"You got a real nice view, too," Benny mentioned.

"I guess," David replied, spinning around to look out the window. The view from his new office peered right over the top of the Texas Capitol. "Believe it or not, Benny, I don't get to spend much time looking out this window. My face is always buried in paperwork."

"Too bad. Life is short. You need to stop and smell the roses."

David smiled. First, Thomas. Now, Benny. Why was everyone ganging up on him lately? As Benny devoured the Chinese food, they made some small talk about the other guys at the Camp. David began to get some background info on each of his new friends: Doc, Curly, Elvis, Shifty, and Larue. Jen was right in that each of the guys had faced a serious loss of family connection at some point that had pushed him to the streets. For a few of them, like Benny, this loss had happened a long time ago, and they never had fully recovered.

"You mind if I ask about your family?" David said to Benny.

The old man had never openly mentioned anything, so David was hesitant to ask him directly about it. He figured there might be a lot of pain there somewhere. Chewing, Benny considered the question for a long moment.

"I had a wife," he said. "I lost her to cancer a long time ago."

"I'm real sorry to hear that."

He nodded, stuffed his mouth with fried rice. "She was a good woman. Took real good care of me, even though I wasn't much of a husband to her all those years. I regret that now." He sighed, stared at his food, added, "I regret a lot of things."

"Any children?" David asked.

Benny slowly nodded. "One. A daughter."

Benny didn't expound on that, so David didn't push him. Instead, he tried to balance the conversation by talking about his own family. "I lost my father when I was a kid. Car wreck."

Benny shook his head. "Tough for a boy to lose his father so young."

"Yeah, then I lost my mother to heart failure when I was seventeen."

Benny looked up at him with sad eyes. "Damn, son, I'm real sorry. That's a shame. Amazing you turned out to be such a good man after something like that."

"I'm not a good man, Benny. I'm not sure what I am anymore."

Benny immediately waved that off. "Nonsense! There is *a lot* of good inside you. I've seen it with my own eyes. The boys all see it. Even Jen Cantwell sees it."

Benny gave him a sly wink. David smiled.

"She's a real sweet gal, that Jen," Benny added. "She's helped a lot of hurting people."

"She lost her brother on the streets a couple of years ago."

Benny nodded. "I tried to help Jack. But the demons were too much for him. He was a good kid. A veteran, like so many of us. That was a real tragedy."

"Based off what I saw at the memorial service the other day, it sounds like these streets are filled with tragedy all year long."

"Yes, they are." Benny put his plate over to the side. "That's actually one of the reasons I wanted to talk with you tonight. I could use your help."

"Of course, Benny. What do you need?"

The old man pulled a couple of sheets of folded paper out of his trench coat pocket. Smoothing them out, he placed them on top of the desk for David to view more easily. The first was an online printout from a Craigslist ad about a local piece of property that was currently for sale. Twenty acres of undeveloped land out near the airport. The current price tag for the property was $120,000. David wondered why Benny had the listing.

"I'm interested in this property," Benny said, placing a crooked finger on the paper. "Do you know much about real estate acquisition?"

"A little," David said, curious. "What do you mean by *interested*?"

"I want to purchase the land."

David looked up at his new friend. He expected to see a funny smile form on the man's weathered face, as if he were telling a joke, but Benny just sat there looking intently at the paper on the desk. Was he serious? He couldn't be—this was crazy. David recalled discovering the thousands of dollars in cash in Benny's dirty old sock, which he still had a lot of questions about, but this was on a different level altogether. A hundred and twenty thousand dollars? Still, he didn't want to come right out and potentially embarrass the old man.

"What're you going to do with twenty acres?"

This time, a smile did form on the man's face. "I'm going to build a village on it. Let me show you." He smoothed out a second sheet of paper, where he'd drawn a meticulous diagram that looked a lot like a community map of sorts. Benny stood, hovered over the paper, and started pointing out different things on the map. "It'll have a place here for camping tents, but it will also have a section over here for real homes, like all those tiny homes you see on TV these days. Nothing fancy. But real homes with four walls, floors, and ceilings, where a man can lock up his possessions and sleep in a real bed at night. I plan to build dozens of these tiny homes. Over here, I want to build a bathhouse with real plumbing that has several private showers and toilets." He then pointed to the middle of the page. "Right here, I want this to be a community center. A place where everyone can gather, where we can hold church and have fellowship, with a real kitchen installed, where we can cook up a lot of good food. This here is the centerpiece of the village."

It dawned on David that the drawing was a glorified version of the Camp. Benny's wrinkled eyes lit up like fireworks as he described in detail his vision for the community. David found it sweet—if not ludicrous. With the proposed purchase of the twenty-acre property, the development of the land, and all the complex construction costs involved, Benny's little dream village would probably cost several million dollars. Still, sitting there staring at the old man, David had never seen Benny look more excited. David could tell this was somehow *very* real to him. He didn't have the heart to tell Benny he couldn't imagine how he'd pull this off.

Benny looked up at him. "Can you help me, Shep? I realize there'll be a lot to this, with the purchasing of the property, the city permits, all the meetings with different land developers and construction companies. I figure I'm going to need a really sharp lawyer wearing a nice suit to help me pull this all together. Otherwise, no one will take me seriously."

"Sure, Benny. I'll do whatever I can to help."

Benny seemed overjoyed to hear him say that. "See, you *are* a good man."

"I'm trying." David introduced a new topic just to see what the old man had to say about it. "Let's talk about funding for your village."

Benny nodded, a pensive look crossing his face. "Yes, it's going to cost a lot of money."

"Exactly."

"I need your help with that, too," Benny admitted.

David figured the old man was about to ask if David could help raise the money among all his rich lawyer friends and their clients. He dreaded having to tell Benny that his lawyer friends—if he could even call them that—probably couldn't care less. He'd be lucky to raise $100 around the office. Hell, if he even tried, Lyons would likely tear into him.

Benny didn't ask him to raise any money. Instead, he asked, "What do you know about offshore numbered accounts?"

David tilted his head. "Well, I know wealthy people sometimes use them to be discreet with money and with their direct connection to it."

"Are they illegal?"

"Not necessarily. Why do you ask?"

"I need your help getting one set up."

David sighed. A secret numbered account? How far was he supposed to go with this conversation? At some point, he didn't feel like he was doing Benny any favors by entertaining all this nonsense. He again thought about the cash stuffed in Benny's sock. "Well, Benny, we'd have to be talking about *a lot* of money to pursue opening a bank account like that. And I don't mean a couple thousand dollars."

"Right, right," Benny agreed. "Would a million dollars do the trick?"

"Well, certainly."

Benny again didn't flinch. "So, can you help me set up a numbered account? It would really mean a lot to me *and* the boys."

David stared at the old man. Every part of his face was pleading with him. Even if it was a fantasy, David just couldn't say no to him right now. "Sure. I'll help."

TWENTY-THREE

Two days later, a private plane touched down in Austin in the dark. The sun wouldn't be up for a few more hours. The pilot shuttled the plane over to a private hangar, where a black Suburban with heavily tinted windows sat idly waiting. Grabbing his travel bag, Frank Hodges stepped off the plane, stretched, looked around, and descended the short stairs. He'd slept well during the flight. The plane had picked him up late last night in Sao Paolo, where Frank had been enjoying beach time with Maria, his curvy young girlfriend, who still had family in Brazil. His client had called with an all-out emergency. They needed him back *right now*.

Annoyed, because his client had been sloppy the first time around by choosing to dismiss him before the job was complete, Frank gave him a hefty price tag. Four times what he'd normally ask to drop everything and jump on a plane. His client immediately agreed to wire the full amount to his account. It was hard to turn down a desperate client with such deep pockets. Maria wasn't pleased. He'd already promised her he'd take the whole month off. She'd pouted the whole time he'd packed his bag. So he'd upped his next offer to her. When he finished this job, he'd give her two uninterrupted months *and* a trip to Greece. She seemed happy with that.

Climbing into the back of the Suburban, Frank found his client waiting for him in the black leather seats. Even at four in the morning, the man wore a suit and tie and was all business. There were no cordial greetings. As the driver of the Suburban eased the vehicle out of the hangar, his client opened his briefcase and handed him a copy of an anonymous email they'd apparently received the day before—the source of their sudden panic.

"One million?" Frank whistled, reading the brief email. As he'd expected, the $10,000 cash drop six weeks ago was simply a test—whoever was behind all this was now going for the full amount.

"Do you think it could be Benjamin Dugan?" his client asked.

Frank shrugged. "We'll have to check everything out."

"It has to be him," his client said, sighing. Staring out the SUV window, he added, "He's the only one left."

Frank grimaced at those words. He knew what that meant. It didn't sit well. But with enough money wired to his account to take up to a full year off, he decided he would finish the job and then have nothing else to do with this client. "I'll need full access to everything to track this guy down. You understand? I can't be handcuffed."

"You'll have it. We need this finished."

TWENTY-FOUR

That whole week, David began secretly researching everything that Nick Carlson had been working on right before his suicide, trying to figure out the mysterious "client" who may have been at the center of his tense text exchange with Lyons—and the one he'd mentioned in passing to his girlfriend regarding potential blackmail. Nick's client list was long, as he'd been actively involved in more than thirty open matters. David went through the clients one by one, looking for hints of something odd. He found nothing.

He called the police department and asked to speak with the detective who had handled Nick's suicide case. He gave the detective a false name, said he was an attorney handling Nick's estate, and he began poking around to see if there was any suspicion of foul play. The detective assured him that the suicide was open-and-shut. Nick had taken an extension cord from his garage, roped it around a hanging beam in his living room, tied the cord around his neck, stood on a kitchen stool, and then finished himself off. Estimated time of death was between ten p.m. and midnight. The girlfriend found him the next day around noon and called the police. She'd told the detective that Nick had been under a tremendous amount of work stress, which confirmed the basics of what they'd found in Nick's suicide note. The detective said Nick was really drunk when he killed himself. The coroner tested his blood alcohol concentration at .18. When David questioned the detective on a man's ability to concoct a hanging system of this sort while being so intoxicated, the detective began to get defensive and irritated. At that point, David quickly thanked him for the information and hung up.

By the end of the week, David was questioning everything. Maybe he was wrong. Maybe he hadn't really seen the white-haired man outside Nick's house. Maybe it had been someone else.

Maybe there really was nothing more to Nick's suicide.

That sure would make David's life easier.

TWENTY-FIVE

The buzzing on his nightstand startled David awake. He stared bleary-eyed at the digital clock. Two in the morning? Who the hell was calling him right now? He'd only been asleep for maybe an hour after pulling another late night at the office. He reached over, somehow found his cell phone in the dark of the bedroom. Holding it up, he didn't recognize the number. He cursed whoever was on the other end, hit "Ignore," and then tried to curl back up under the warm bedcovers. A new round of buzzing started almost immediately. David grabbed the phone again. Same damn number. *Come on!*

He answered with a gruff, "What!"

"Shep, this you?"

David thought he recognized the voice but couldn't immediately place it. The guy called him Shep. The Camp? It wasn't Benny's voice. "Yeah, it's me. Who is this?"

"It's Doc, from the Camp. You remember me?"

David pushed himself up a little on the bed. His head was fuzzy. Doc was calling him? "Yeah, sure, Doc. What . . . why're you calling at this hour?"

He heard Doc exhale deeply. "It's Benny. He's . . . uh . . . he's dead, man. Benny is dead."

Doc's words hit him like a hard slap across the face. David suddenly felt alert.

"Wait . . . what? Benny?"

"Someone shot him dead tonight," Doc said, the emotion clear in his shaky voice. "We don't know what all happened. But Benny is dead, and Larue is in police custody."

David swung his feet to the carpet, turned on his nightstand lamp. Benny was dead? Larue was in police custody? His mind was swirling. "Larue shot Benny?"

"I don't know," Doc declared. "That's what the cops are saying. But we can't find out any more information from them. No one will talk to us. But it doesn't make any sense. Larue missed his shift today. He had kitchen duty at the Camp and never showed up for it, so we were all out searching for him. I guess Benny found him first, and then something really bad happened. We can't believe it. We're all in shock."

"Where are you, Doc?"

"Outside the Travis County Jail, where they're holding Larue."

"Stay put. I'll be there in ten minutes."

Hanging up, David sat there for a moment. Benny was dead? It couldn't be true. There had to be another explanation. Rushing to his closet, he threw on a pair of jeans and a T-shirt.

David found the boys huddled closely together on the sidewalk right outside the downtown county jail. Doc, Curly, Shifty, Elvis, and several others were all there. Everyone was clearly distraught. There were a lot of red eyes and looks of disbelief. But they were glad to see David, as if he were somehow in a position to straighten out this whole thing for them. However, if Benny was dead, what could he really do?

"Thanks for coming," Doc said.

"Tell me exactly what happened."

Curly stepped forward. "I heard the police cars, so I ran over to Sixth Street. A big group of people had started to gather on the sidewalk. They were all saying some homeless guy had been shot in the alley by a street kid. That's when I saw the cops shoving Larue in the back of a police car. Larue saw me, too, and started yelling over to me that Benny was dead. But that's all he got out before they slammed the door shut and raced off with him."

David turned back to Doc. "Could Larue have done it?"

Doc shook his head. "No way. Benny was like a father to him."

Shifty stepped forward. "Can you do something, Shep? You're a lawyer, right?"

"Not that kind of lawyer."

"Well, you're the only damn lawyer we got!" Elvis blurted out.

"Take it easy, Elvis," Doc said, before turning back to David. "We're all a bit on edge."

David felt all their eyes on him, pleading for him to do something. "Anyone know Larue's full name?" David asked.

Doc knew it and gave him the kid's legal name.

Sighing, David said, "Okay, let me see what I can do."

Walking into the county jail, David immediately felt out of place. First, he was a corporate attorney, not a criminal attorney. Second, he was wearing blue jeans and a T-shirt, not one of his power suits. Would anyone even take him seriously? Still, the boys outside really needed him. After passing through a security checkpoint, David walked up to the front counter of the jail and signed in with a female deputy who seemed to be operating on autopilot. After showing her his State Bar card, he said he was there to see his client: Lawrence Luther James. She punched a few buttons on her computer and instructed him to have a seat.

David sat in the small lobby, feeling uneasy. There were uniformed officers and other police authorities coming in and out. The lobby was stuffed with what he imagined were mostly family members or friends of those who'd been tossed into jail tonight. Maybe a couple of lawyers, too, he thought, as he spotted two guys in cheap suits with scuffed briefcases. They probably had clients locked up on drunk-and-disorderly charges. He doubted either of them was there waiting to see a client who'd just been arrested on potential murder charges.

What the hell had he gotten himself into?

After he'd waited for nearly fifteen minutes, a secured door opened to his right, and another uniformed deputy called out the name of his client. David popped up, hurried over to the door. Without saying much, the deputy led him down a long hallway and then opened a door to a room with several private booths—the same thing he'd seen in movies, where attorneys sit down to talk to clients through a clear protective partition.

"Number four," the deputy said, shutting the door behind him.

The other booths were currently empty. David walked over to number four, sat in a stiff metal chair, wondered how this was all supposed to work. No one was sitting on the other side of the partition. David took a second to try to gather his thoughts, figure out what he was even going to say to Larue. He felt overwhelmed by the moment. Benny was dead? Seconds later, a door on the other side opened, and a deputy led Larue over to David's private booth. Larue was already wearing the standard black-and-gray-striped county jail jumpsuit. The kid looked like he was limping badly. His eyes were also swollen. Although clearly distraught, Larue seemed relieved to see a familiar face sitting across the partition from him.

David picked up the private booth phone; Larue did the same.

"What you doing here, Shep?" Larue asked.

"I'm here for you. Doc called me."

"I didn't do it, man. I keep telling 'em that. No one will believe me. I'm innocent!"

"Slow down," David urged him. "Just tell me what happened."

"I was hanging out in the alley behind Pete's tonight. I do it a couple of times a week. Listening to the piano battle going on through the crack in the back door. Suddenly, I hear something up the alley. A man's voice. I peek out from behind a stack of boxes. That's when I see Benny standing there and another man approaching him from behind. Benny turns around to look at the guy, and then this dude pulls out a gun and just shoots him straight up. But they weren't loud gunshots. The gun had one of them silencer things on it. Benny drops and doesn't move again. This dude starts looking around, so I push myself all the way behind the boxes to hide. Then the guy bolts. I freak out and run over to Benny, trying to shake him awake. But Benny ain't moving. Then another dude comes out the back of Pete's, sees me on top of Benny. I got blood all over my hands. The guy yells about calling the cops. I panicked, Shep. It looks bad, a black kid like me and a dead old white dude. So I tried to run. But I heard a bad pop in my knee and fell. The same knee I jacked up two years ago playing ball. I kept trying to run, but the pain was so damn bad, I could hardly make it out of the alley. By then, it was too late. Cops were on top of me, shoving my face into the concrete."

David was stunned. Someone had shot Benny? He could still see remnants of the dried-up blood on Larue's big hands. Benny's dried-up blood. *Damn.*

"How do you even know what a silencer is, Larue?"

"Used to play that *Hitman* shooter video game all the dang time. The gun in this dude's hand looked and sounded just like the gun from that game."

David wasn't sure what to make of that claim. A gun with a silencer? That seemed ridiculous. No wonder the cops didn't believe him. He could only think that Larue had an overactive imagination. Still, that didn't mean the kid deserved to be locked up. David thought about the serious wad of cash Benny had been carrying around in his sock.

"Listen, I need you to think really hard about this, Larue. Did the guy take anything off Benny after shooting him like that?"

Larue seemed adamant. "He didn't take a dang thing. Dude just shot Benny straight up without saying another word to him. Then the dude stood over Benny, like making sure he was dead and all, before he ran his ass out of there."

"Could it have been a robbery that got interrupted?"

"Nah, man. The dude had plenty of time if he really wanted to steal something from Benny. He wasn't robbing him, man. Just killing him."

"You get a good look at the guy?"

"Yeah, man. About your height and build. Black leather jacket."

"What about his age?"

"Dude, I don't know. Older than you. But not too old."

"What else, Larue? He have an accent or anything?"

"No. Talked normal."

"Hair color? Beard?"

"No beard. Short white hair."

That comment sent a cold chill down David's spine. "White hair?"

"Yeah, Shep."

"You're sure?"

"Yeah. Buzz cut. Like an army dude."

David felt his heart pounding in his chest. Black jacket? Buzz-cut white hair? "You told all of this to the police?"

"Yeah, man. I told 'em *everything*. They ain't having none of it. They just keep threatening me, saying my only chance is to tell 'em where I ditched the gun." Larue cursed, his eyes growing wet. "Man, I did this to Benny, Shep. I forgot about my kitchen shift tonight. Just slipped my dang mind. Benny was prolly looking for me, to see if I was okay." Larue was getting more distraught. "Benny was prolly in that alley because of me. And now he's dead, man. I can't believe it. He's dead."

"You can't blame yourself," David said, trying to settle the kid down. "It won't bring Benny back."

"What am I gonna do? They got my ass locked up. I ain't got nobody."

David swallowed. "You got me, okay? I'm going to work on getting you out of here."

"Dang, man, thank you!"

"Don't thank me yet. I haven't done anything." David wondered what the hell Marty Lyons was going to say if he found out David was representing a homeless street kid who was about to be charged with murder. "Are you badly hurt, Larue?"

"Yeah, man, my knee hurts like hell, and they ain't giving me a dang thing for it."

"I'll get that fixed ASAP."

"Seriously, I owe you, Shep."

"You don't owe me anything. Listen, I owe you. I was a complete ass to you on the sidewalk outside of my building the other day. You deserved better from me. I'm sorry."

"Nah, man. You get me out of this, all is forgiven. I swear."

TWENTY-SIX

The Travis County Medical Examiner's Office was on Springdale Road. David explained to the morgue attendant that he was the attorney for a victim who'd likely been brought in a few hours ago—Benjamin Dugan, a sixtysomething man with a gray beard. Benny had given him his legal name at the office the other night in order for David to establish the offshore numbered account. David had set up the account the following day with a bank in the Caymans, although it would become active only after an initial deposit. Based on his first experience with Benny while inside his condo, David wasn't sure if the old man ever carried any real identification on him. As expected, the attendant didn't have anyone by the name of Benjamin Dugan officially listed in the system. But he confirmed they had an unidentified older man brought in tonight who matched David's description.

David was led into a cold and antiseptic room. There were metal slots all along one wall where he supposed dead bodies were stored. There were two bodies already out on tables, both of them covered in white sheets. The attendant walked David over to the second table, where he pulled the sheet down off the face, as if it were no big deal. David had found himself hoping that he somehow wouldn't see Benny's face beneath the sheet—that this might all still be some huge mistake—but that faint hope was immediately dashed. It was Benny.

David felt short of breath at the sight of his friend lying there.

"This your client?"

David nodded. "It's him."

"That's good. That'll help us. He had no identification on him. We need you to fill out some paperwork to better help us process the body, if you don't mind."

"Sure. What happens next?"

"We contact the family and release him to their preferred funeral home."

"He has a daughter. But you probably won't be able to find her."

"Then he'll be released to a facility that handles unclaimed and unidentified bodies for the county, where he'll be cremated and buried in a county cemetery with others like him."

"Can you release him to his attorney?"

"Probably, if there's no family available."

"I don't want him buried in a cemetery with other unclaimed bodies, okay? I'll take care of the funeral home and burial myself."

"Suit yourself."

"What about personal effects?" David asked.

"If there's no family, we'll release them to you. You can pick them up tomorrow around noon."

"Okay, thanks."

"You want a few minutes alone with him?"

David nodded. The attendant wandered off, leaving David alone in the cold room. He stared down at the face of his friend. Although Benny's eyes were closed, he looked really peaceful. He didn't look like a man who had been probably frightened before getting shot. This moment felt surreal—the old man had just been inside his office a few nights ago, munching on Chinese food, and talking about all his dreams. Now he was lying on a cold table with bullet holes in his chest.

David kept expecting Benny to open his eyes, give him that perfect stain-toothed smile, hop up off that gurney, and say, "Come on, Shep, let's go get some blueberry cobbler!" But the old man never moved.

Benny was gone. David couldn't believe it.

For a moment, he thought about Larue's story and the white-haired man. It had to be the same guy whom he'd seen with Lyons. Probably the same guy who'd been outside Nick's house that night. All his fears about Nick came rushing back to the surface. Who the hell was this guy? And why would he shoot and kill an old homeless man? It didn't make any sense at all. But it scared the hell out of him.

David hadn't prayed too often since his mom had died. It had always been too much of a struggle. But considering how Benny had been such an openly God-fearing man, he felt it appropriate to fumble through something now, in this quiet moment. Benny deserved that from him. He put his hand on the old man's cold shoulder, bowed his head, and with wet eyes, asked God to take Benny to a much better place. That sweet village in the sky. The eternal home for dry bones.

TWENTY-SEVEN

David knocked on the door of the small duplex.

He felt uneasy standing there, at three thirty in the morning, but he couldn't stand the thought of returning to his lonely condo. He needed to talk to someone tonight. Not just any someone—he needed to talk to the *right* someone. He knocked again, more firmly. He finally saw a light flicker on in the window next to the front door. Seconds later, he heard locks being unfastened, and then Jen's tired and confused face was staring at him through the door crack. Her hair was a disheveled mess, and she wore a gray T-shirt and black pajama pants.

"David? What're you doing here?"

"Benny is dead."

Her eyes widened. She quickly pulled open the door. "What happened?"

"He was killed on the streets tonight."

"No!" Jen exclaimed. "How?"

He shook his head. "It's a long story. Can I come in?"

"Of course!"

She led him into a tiny living room with a red sofa and a brown swivel chair. It was the exact opposite of Melissa's home, where everything matched perfectly. The walls were nearly barren. She invited him to sit on the sofa, and then she sat in the swivel chair with her knees to her chest.

"What happened, David?"

"Someone shot him in an alley on Sixth Street."

Jen put her hand to her mouth. "Why?"

David told her about Larue and his visit with the kid in the county jail a few hours ago. He left out the potential connection of the white-haired man to everything he'd discovered at the firm. There was no reason to add fuel to the drama tonight.

"Poor Benny," Jen said.

"I'm still shocked. I can't shake it."

"Are you going to be Larue's lawyer?"

"Yes, the kid has no other help. The boys can't help him."

"That's really good of you."

"Maybe or maybe not. We'll see. But for damn sure, I won't let the kid go down without a fight, I can promise you that. I owe Larue. And I owe Benny at least that much."

"I just can't believe it," Jen said, shaking her head. "Benny was a true hero out there on the streets. It's so tragic. He's going to be missed by so many."

They both sat there in silence for a long moment. David stood, not wanting to overstay his welcome. He already felt a little better after sharing the heartache with Jen.

"I guess I should probably get going," he said.

"Uh, no, sir, you're not going *anywhere!*"

He looked over at Jen, who frowned at him.

"David, you can't come over here in the middle of the night, tell me that Benny was shot and killed by some crazy guy with a gun, and then just bolt out the door. Are you kidding me? I'll stare at the ceiling the rest of the night, completely freaked out. I'm not sure if you noticed, but I don't exactly live in the nicest part of town."

"You want me to stay?"

"You're either staying or taking me with you."

A small smile crossed his lips. "Okay, I'll stay."

He glanced over toward a door that looked like the only bedroom.

Jen read his mind, rolled her eyes. "You can sleep on the sofa, Romeo."

TWENTY-EIGHT

David avoided the office the entire morning. He couldn't stomach the thought of sitting at his desk and billing one mind-numbing hour of work after his friend had been killed in a dirty alley. At noon, he picked up Benny's personal items from the medical examiner's office—a clear Ziploc bag filled with basically the same gear that Benny had with him the first night they'd met: a Bible, a bottle of water, cigarettes, a lighter, loose change, eight dollars in cash, a package of peanut butter crackers, and a worn Louis L'Amour paperback. There was no sign of the marked envelope with the $100 bills. If Larue had been correct, and Benny's killer had not stolen anything from him, David wondered what his friend had done with the money.

After making official arrangements to have Benny's body transferred to a funeral home, David and Jen worked with the director to schedule a burial service for the following morning. Jen suggested the sooner the better—word was already out on the streets, and everyone was in deep mourning. All were eager to pay their fondest respects to a man who had meant so much. David had asked Doc if he knew anything about possibly finding Benny's estranged daughter, but Doc didn't have a clue. He said Benny *never* talked about her.

At two, David visited Larue again in the county jail. Thankfully, the kid had received some pain medication. Larue said his knee was more tolerable but still hurt like hell. His eyes were even more red and puffy than the previous night. He again pleaded with David to help him get out of this desperate mess. David explained to Larue that they would stand before a judge in two days and find out what charges were being brought against him, as well as try to get him released on bail. Although David knew bail was a long shot if murder charges were indeed brought against Larue, he tried to reassure the kid that everything was going to be okay. Inside, David wasn't so sure—could he really somehow defend Larue against a murder charge if this went all the way to trial? Would the firm even allow him the chance?

David's cell phone began buzzing incessantly by midafternoon—mostly calls from Marty Lyons, who clearly wasn't happy that his protégé was not only not at the office but not dialing the partner immediately back with a worthy excuse. David clicked "Ignore" to each call. He knew he couldn't talk to Lyons today. He'd probably say something he'd really regret. *Who's the white-haired guy, boss? A killer? Are you somehow the reason Nick Carlson is dead? What the hell is going on?* Questions like that would open Pandora's box. David wasn't quite ready to do that yet. Not until he could get his mind around all this. And he couldn't stand the thought of Lyons berating him right now.

David felt numb most of the day. It was still so hard to believe that Benny was actually gone. So he was grateful when Doc called him, said the boys at the Camp had decided to throw a grand party in Benny's honor that night, and he invited David and Jen to come. While sad at the reason behind the invite, Jen was also excited to finally see the sacred place for herself. After picking up Jen, David stopped by Whole Foods, where he filled up an entire small cooler with stacks of fresh steaks, and then they drove over to East Austin. They parked along the same curb that David had on his first visit to the woods with Benny. This time, Curly was standing there at the edge, waiting for them. David had told

Doc there was no way he'd remember how to navigate his way back to the Camp.

After exchanging warm greetings with Curly, David grabbed the cooler, and they followed the man and his flashlight into the woods, up and down several small hills, and over the creek with the makeshift bridge. Curly mentioned to Jen that everyone was especially excited to have her visit them. The boys had spent hours cleaning up the place and making sure it was all perfect for her. David and Jen shared a small smile.

As they entered the clearing for the Camp, David could see and hear the energy up ahead. The party had already started. The boys were jamming around the campfire to upbeat music. They'd also plugged strands of bright white Christmas lights into a generator and had hung them throughout all the trees. The Christmas lights really brought the Camp to life. He watched Jen's face closely as she took it all in for the first time. He'd never seen her smile so big, the white lights sparkling in her big green eyes.

The boys erupted in loud cheers upon seeing David and Jen. They dropped whatever they were doing and rushed over, embracing both of them with the same warmth he'd felt from them from the beginning. David gave the cooler loaded with steaks to Elvis, who hauled it off to the kitchen canopy. Shifty immediately tucked Jen's arm around his and began the grand tour. Red started up a new jam session with his guitar—"When We All Get to Heaven"—and the boys began dancing around and clapping again.

David just stood there, soaking it all up. Benny would have loved this party. He clearly loved these men. He couldn't help but think about the last time he was alone with Benny, inside his office just a few nights ago, when the old man had shared his plans for purchasing twenty acres of land and turning them into something special for these guys. Benny had been so excited about it. And now the old man was gone. David's eyes grew moist. Looking around at this ragtag group who had become his new friends—maybe his *only* friends—David felt like he'd give just about anything to see Benny's dream somehow become reality.

Doc came over to David. "How's the kid?"

David sighed. "Hanging in there, I guess. We'll know a lot more in two days."

"Larue's tough. He'll be all right."

"Were you able to start getting word out about the service tomorrow?"

"You bet. Word travels faster than email out on the streets. I expect a good turnout. Benny was loved and respected." He shook his head, exhaled deeply. "Still so hard to believe. But the boys seem energized by the idea of throwing a party tonight rather than sitting around here and staring sadly at each other."

"Thanks for inviting us."

Doc patted him on the back. "You're one of us now, Shep. You belong here."

David said thanks, and he really meant it. They watched the singing and dancing for a bit. Red moved on to a raucous version of "Oh Happy Day!" David could smell the steaks being cooked over the campfire grill. The boys were excited to bite into them.

David leaned over to Doc. "You do anything with Benny's things yet?"

"Nah, haven't touched them. None of us wants to go anywhere near his tent right now—that might make this all too real. I'm not ready for that. Might not be ready for a while, to tell you the truth. Benny was my best friend."

"You mind if I do?" David asked Doc. "I'd like to see if there is anything to help me somehow find his daughter."

"Not at all. Come on."

David followed Doc around the campfire and down the lantern-lit trail. Across the way, he noticed Shifty and Jen standing near the wooden benches by the outdoor chapel. Shifty was putting on some kind of show, his hands waving all around in the air, and Jen just kept laughing at him. She looked over toward David. Their eyes connected, and they shared another smile. He was falling fast for her. Jen was unlike anyone he'd ever known—although she didn't exactly fit into his shiny new world at the law firm. He wasn't sure what to do about that just yet.

Hell, he wasn't sure about a lot of things right now.

Doc stepped up into the small circle of tents that Shifty had mentioned, on his last visit, belonged to the elders. Doc pulled down a lantern from a hook on the tree, turned on the light, gave it to David. "This is Benny's," he said, nodding toward a green two-man tent. "Or *was* Benny's, I guess. I'll be over by the campfire if you need me."

"Thanks, Doc."

As Doc walked away, David knelt, put his hand on the tent zipper. It felt weird to be the first one to enter Benny's tent after his death. He tugged on the zipper, created a crawl space, and then slipped inside the tent with the lantern. It smelled a bit like Benny—a mix of body odor, cigarettes, *and* blueberry cobbler. He found a rolled-up black sleeping bag and a small pillow in the middle of the tent. It was hard to believe the old man had spent nearly every night of the past six years sleeping on the hard ground while inside a camping tent. No wonder Benny had snoozed so hard that first night on top of David's comfortable bed.

There were two small gray duffel bags in one corner of the tent; in the opposite corner was the black duffel bag Benny had carried with him the night he'd visited David at the office. Everything was nice and tidy. Benny didn't have a lot of loose items. It looked like he was always packed and ready to go at a moment's notice. Perhaps that's how you had to live while on the streets—always ready to bolt.

David pulled the two gray duffel bags over in front of him. Unzipping the first one, he found a stack of clothes that were all folded neatly. A pair of blue jeans and khaki work pants. Two white T-shirts. Three pairs of underwear. A green military-style jacket. A pair of worn-out old tennis shoes. Two rolls of socks, both of which had serious holes in the toes. David shook his head. Knowing Benny, he'd probably given the new socks David had left for him that first night to another street friend. David also found a small toiletry bag filled with everyday items: toothbrush, toothpaste, deodorant, comb, bar of soap, and a small first-aid kit.

David unzipped the second gray duffel bag. Inside, he discovered two long-sleeve, button-down flannel shirts. A set of playing cards. A collection of paperback novels. Tom Clancy. John Grisham. Louis L'Amour. Two flashlights with extra batteries. A set of thick work gloves. Two black knit caps. A brown scarf. A heavy-duty silver thermos. Several sets of plastic cutlery all rolled up tightly with a rubber band. And a big leather Bible, the pages all thoroughly marked up with a pen. In the back, David discovered a small photograph of a young woman holding a baby girl. He turned the photograph over and found a name and date scribbled on the back: *Cassie Ray, 8-13-08*. He stared at the face of the woman. Could the photo be of Benny's daughter and perhaps a granddaughter? He didn't necessarily see Benny in her features. The date on the back of the photo meant the baby girl would now be around eleven years old. It was definitely something worth looking into further.

Reaching into the other corner of the tent, he grabbed the black duffel bag that Benny had with him at his office the other night. He unzipped it, took a peek inside. His eyes narrowed. The first thing he noticed was a black Nikon camera with a long lens attached. He lifted it out and examined it. The camera looked brand-new and expensive. What was Benny doing with a really nice camera with a high-powered lens? Setting it aside, he searched the bag further. He pulled out a black metal kit about the size of a shoebox. He flipped two latches on the end and opened it. Inside, he found what looked like a black electronic dashboard of some sort, with a small TV screen. The topside of the kit had thick gray foam with cutouts that held three identical small black boxes. One black box was missing. He pulled out one small box and studied it. The device looked like a tiny camera of sorts. What the hell was all this? He'd never seen anything like it.

Setting the black kit to the side, David dug around in the bottom of the bag and pulled out a thick brown accordion file wrapped up tightly with several rubber bands. He pulled off the rubber bands, opened the file, and searched through the contents. He grabbed a clear Ziploc bag that held a stack of receipts clipped together. One receipt listed the purchase of the Nikon camera about six weeks ago at Austin Camera & Imaging. The price was a whopping $700. Another receipt listed a purchase for nearly $1,200 worth of equipment at a place called Austin Spy Shop. David looked over at the black metal kit. Spy gear? What the hell was Benny doing? He found more miscellaneous receipts, including two from a taxi service for around the same time frame, with each listing a fee of about $250. They were from the same day. One in the morning, one in the evening. Where had Benny gone that had cost him $500?

In another section of the accordion file, David noticed an old photograph that showed seven young men standing on a dock somewhere, all wearing navy uniforms. David immediately recognized the eyes of the first guy on the left. They were Benny's eyes, only from probably fortysomething years ago. The old man had once mentioned serving in the navy—the school of hard knocks, he'd said. David turned over the photograph, hoping to find more information on the back. There were seven first names scribbled: *Benny, Charlie, Sammy, Marvin, Cliff, Jerry, and Ned.* Beneath the names were the words *Atsugi, Japan. 1977.*

Continuing to search through the accordion file, David pulled out another manila folder. Inside was a printout of a recent magazine article from *Texas Lawyer*, dated March of the current year. The article listed the names of three newly hired litigation associates at Hunter & Kellerman and showed law school photographs. David stared at three different photos: William Tidmore's, Claire Monroe's, and his. For some reason, Benny had circled David's photo with a red marker. Behind the *Texas Lawyer* article, David found even more printed-out news articles from other publications. He shook his head. They were all articles about him. *What the hell?*

There was a story from the *Odessa American* about his high school football team's playoff run his senior year. The article mentioned David overcoming tragedy earlier that year when his mother had suddenly passed away. There was a story from the *Abilene Reporter-News* that mentioned David's knee injury during spring practice his freshman year at ACU. There were two different articles from *Stanford Lawyer Magazine* that highlighted David's mock-trial victories at different competitions. Why did Benny have all these different articles about him?

Then David found something truly stunning.

In the very back of the accordion file, David discovered a copy of a news article about a litigation matter involving a company called the Upella Group, which David recognized as one of Lyons's clients. The Upella Group was a global business consulting company. An accounting firm out of Florida called Zeitler was suing the Upella Group for mismanaged consulting that they claimed led to a loss of millions of dollars. The article directly mentioned Marty Lyons and Nick Carlson as the attorneys representing Upella in the matter. Both names had been highlighted in yellow. Behind the news article, David found a manila folder that held about a dozen eight-by-ten-inch photographs. They looked like surveillance photos of two men standing together by a car in a parking lot somewhere. One of them was Marty Lyons. The other man wore a black leather jacket and had short white hair.

TWENTY-NINE

David and Jen were back inside her duplex. It was nearing midnight. It had taken everything within David to not say goodbye to the boys at the Camp immediately and rush out of there upon his discoveries inside Benny's tent. All his findings from Benny's black duffel bag were now spread out on Jen's dining table: the surveillance photos, the news articles, the navy photo, the stack of receipts, the Nikon camera, and the black spy kit. David had spilled everything to Jen on the drive over. All his suspicions about Nick's death, the white-haired man, and his boss's potential involvement. It shocked him even more to say it all out loud.

Jen examined the surveillance photos showing Marty Lyons meeting with the white-haired man. "You really think this could be the guy who killed Benny?"

"Larue said black leather jacket, short white hair, like an army dude."

"You're right, it has to be him," Jen agreed. "Which means Benny somehow knew about the guy who killed him. But how is your boss involved?"

"I don't know yet. I'm familiar with the Upella Group, although I haven't personally worked on any of their case matters. I did some investigating when I was looking into Nick's caseload but didn't see anything unusual with their litigation. I'm going to have to look even deeper—there must be something I missed."

"But you suspect that your friend Nick might have been killed because of his involvement in this situation somehow?"

"I only know that Lyons wanted him to keep his mouth shut. But now I suspect the white-haired guy might have shown up at Nick's house that night to make sure of it."

"This is scary, David."

"I know."

David fiddled with the black kit and tried to figure out how to power up the electronic dashboard with the small TV screen. He pressed a black button in the bottom right of the dashboard, and the lights flashed. A moment later, the small TV screen came to life. It flickered momentarily and then suddenly showed an office space with a massive desk in the middle, as if the video were taken from a hidden camera. The massive desk with the expansive windows behind it was familiar, which made David curse out loud.

"What?" Jen asked.

He turned the kit so that she could see the small TV screen.

"This is inside Marty Lyons's office," David exclaimed.

She squinted at the screen. "Is that a video feed?"

"Yeah, I think so. There's a rolling date and time stamp at the top."

Jen's brow bunched. "How's this even possible?"

"When Benny came to my office a few nights ago, he brought this black duffel bag with him. I left him alone for a few minutes to get him some food. When I got back, Benny was standing inside Lyons's office. He must've planted the hidden camera."

"Why would Benny do that? None of this makes any sense. Why would he do any of this?" she asked, waving her hand at all the items on the table. "We're talking about Benny here—just some homeless street preacher. Not a spy. I've known him for years. He's just an old man who was living in a tent in the woods with some other guys."

"I think there's much more to Benny than we know."

She sighed. "Did he ever say *anything* to you about Marty Lyons?"

"Nothing. But the other night when Benny came to see me, he asked for my help. He said he needed a lawyer. Then he shared this crazy plan with me where he wanted to buy twenty acres of land and develop it into this brand-new village. A safe place for all of the boys and others from the streets. He asked me to help him with the project."

"Help, how?"

"Purchase the land."

Jen frowned. "How was Benny going to buy twenty acres of land?"

"No clue. I obviously didn't take him too seriously. We even talked about how it would cost millions of dollars to develop such a project. Benny asked me to set up an offshore numbered bank account."

"Did you do it?"

"Yes, the next day. But the account only becomes active with an opening wire transfer. Benny and I discussed how it would have to be a significant amount of money."

"You think Benny had money somewhere?"

"No, but I think he was planning to get it somehow."

"You think Benny was at the center of this so-called blackmail that Nick told his girlfriend about?"

"I don't know what to think anymore."

Jen picked up all the articles Benny had printed out about David. She then studied the story from *Texas Lawyer* that listed David as a new litigation hire at Hunter & Kellerman.

"These articles about you were all printed out two months ago," Jen stated. "But you've only known Benny for a few weeks, right?"

"How do you know when they were printed?"

She showed him the bottom of the pages. "They're marked with a printer tagline. You have to pay for printing at the public library."

David stared at the tagline. It was a date before he'd ever even met Benny. He considered that thought for a moment. Benny had already known about him *before* they'd ever had the encounter with the mugger in the alley? How was that possible? Then he thought of something else. He quickly pulled out his phone, opened his web browser.

"What is it?" Jen asked.

"Hold on a sec." David pulled up YouTube. He then did a search for a local used-car dealership called Joe Mitchell's, or Crazy Joe's, as the car dealer called himself in all of his goofy TV commercials—including the one where he was wearing a leotard and wrestling a big muscle-bound guy. That was the commercial that had caught David's attention the other night in the office kitchen. As expected, Crazy Joe had his own YouTube page. David scrolled down and found the recent commercial. He pressed "Play." When Crazy Joe had the muscled guy in a headlock, David paused the video and stared right at the guy's face. Unbelievable. He quickly scanned the credits below the video on the YouTube page and found a name for the wrestler. Clicking on it, he discovered another YouTube page belonging to an actor named Oscar Belfer that showed him in a dozen other local TV commercials.

"He was an actor," David exclaimed, hardly believing it.

"Who was an actor?"

He handed her his phone. "This is the same guy who tried to mug me in the alley the night Benny saved my life. He's just an actor, Jen. He's not a street thug."

"Why would an actor try to mug you?"

"Because Benny hired him to do it."

"No way. Benny? I don't believe it."

David thought about the gash and the real blood on Benny's head that night. That wasn't fake. He'd doctored it up himself. He set his gaze back on the table that was littered with all the bizarre contents from Benny's bag. "Benny had something big at play here. We need to find out what he was doing."

"We *need* to go to the police."

"I can't go to the police yet, Jen. What if I'm wrong about all of this? What if Benny's just a lunatic? What if it's all speculation and no substance? If I go to the police right now and drag Lyons into the middle of all of this, my days at Hunter and Kellerman are over. I can't risk that until we find out what's really going on here with Benny."

THIRTY

Benny was laid to rest in Oakwood Cemetery, located just outside of downtown proper. An easy walk for most of the street community, which is what David and Jen had in mind. David got there early and watched as a big crowd gradually arrived. There were hundreds of somber street folk, as well as dozens more who likely knew Benny through their volunteer work. Doc had been right. Word spread quickly on the streets. David wondered if he'd even have twenty people attend his burial service should he die tomorrow. He doubted that too many associates from the firm would be there; if they did attend, it would be mainly for show. There certainly wouldn't be the same genuine tears he already saw in so many eyes now surrounding him at the gravesite.

Benny had clearly loved people. They loved him back.

The sky was appropriately gray, with hints of rain. David stood close to Jen as the pastor from the Church Under the Bridge gave a heartfelt message of hope in Christ in the midst of the chaos and tragedy of our lives and deaths. The message clearly resonated with the crowd. There were a whole lot of loud "Amens" shouted throughout the message. A woman from the church stood up and sang "Amazing Grace" a cappella. David glanced around him. Most of the crowd slept on benches, in alleys, in shelters, under bridges, in boxes, and in sleeping bags in the woods, but when the singer invited them to join her in the singing of the chorus, damn near the entire group belted out, "That saved a wretch like me . . ."

Jen reached over, clasped his hand in hers. He looked at her. She had her eyes closed and was also singing her heart out. David felt a catch in his throat. Their hands felt good linked together. He took in the whole crowd, his eyes passing over so many dirty faces. Like many moments from the past few weeks, David knew this was one he wouldn't soon forget. Taking a deep breath, he exhaled slowly. He'd arrived in Austin just six weeks ago, ready to conquer the world. Ready to build himself an ivory tower and take great pleasure in all the riches of his new life. A lifelong dream finally realized for the dirt-poor West Texas kid. And, now, everything seemed to be changing—because of Benny. In more ways than one, the old man had unexpectedly swooped into his life and had flipped everything upside down.

Doc stood up, representing the boys from the Camp, and said some meaningful words about their dear friend. Shifty was crying his eyes out. Elvis and Curly had their arms wrapped over each other's shoulders, as if they were holding each other up. Although they had no official record yet of Benny having served in the navy, other than the photograph they'd found in his belongings, David had hired a local musician to play "Taps." As he finished, it began to sprinkle. The pastor quickly ended the service with a prayer. As the crowd dispersed, several folks walked over and set different mementos on top of Benny's casket.

David gave hugs all around to the boys. As the rain started to fall more heavily, David noticed someone standing next to a gray Ford Taurus about fifty yards out on one of the cemetery's internal roads. He hadn't been part of the actual service, but he was watching the crowd intently. David squinted, swallowed.

It was the white-haired man wearing the black leather jacket.

THIRTY-ONE

An hour later, David was sitting in a downtown coffee shop. He'd made contact with the actor, Oscar Belfer, who was in Crazy Joe's TV commercial—the same guy who'd accosted him in the alley a few weeks ago. He was easy to find. The muscle-bound guy had his own crappy acting website. In a brief email exchange, David said he had a job offer but needed to immediately meet in person to discuss it.

Through a front window, David watched as Oscar walked up the sidewalk. David shook his head, couldn't believe the transformation. The guy looked *a lot* different from their last engagement. For one, he was wearing normal clothes—blue jeans, T-shirt, brown sport coat, loafers. There was also no dragon tattoo hissing fire up his neck. It had clearly been a fake.

When the guy entered the coffee shop, David flagged him down from his table near the front window. They shook hands, exchanged quick greetings. The guy eyeballed David a bit, probably trying to place him. Although David would never forget the guy's face, since it had been one of the scariest moments of his life, he doubted the brief encounter had had the same impact on the actor. After all, the alley was dark, and they were only face-to-face for a couple of minutes.

"So what's the job?" the guy asked, sitting across from David.

David pulled up a photo on his phone—the one Jen had taken with him and Benny standing together the other day. He slid his phone in front of Oscar. In a flash, the actor seemed to recognize Benny and then suddenly realized why David looked so familiar to him.

"Remember me?" David asked.

Oscar nodded but clearly didn't know what to say. "I'm not looking for any trouble, man. That was just a job for me. You were never in any real jeopardy."

"Who hired you for the job?"

Oscar put a thick finger on Benny. "The old dude."

David cocked his head. "You're telling me this old man was okay with you slamming him up against a metal dumpster and nearly breaking his skull that night?"

"Yeah, that's exactly what I'm telling you. Beforehand, he told me to not hold back, that it had to look real. Even if he got injured during it."

"What else did he tell you?"

Oscar shrugged. "Not much. He contacted me, said he had a job. We met, and at first, I didn't take him too seriously. I mean, the guy looked like a street bum. But then he put cash on the table in front of me. The old man said he needed me to fake a mugging, to make it all look really scary, but I had to allow him to save the day. He said he was going to jump on me from behind, put me in a choke hold, but that I couldn't go down too easy. We even spent a half hour working through some of the physical logistics. It was a weird job, I'll admit, but I'm a broke actor just trying to survive, man, so I took it."

David sat back in his chair. Benny really had set him up. The old man had staged the entire incident. He'd allowed himself to be beaten to hell in the process. Would Benny really put himself through all that to cultivate a relationship to gain greater access to the firm?

David looked at Oscar. "The old guy ever say why he was doing it?"

"Nope. And I never asked."

"You ever hear from him again?" David said.

Oscar shook his head. "I'm guessing there is no job offer here?"

David took a $100 bill out of his wallet, put it on the table. "Thanks for your time."

THIRTY-TWO

David dropped into his office right at lunch, hoping to avoid an encounter with Marty Lyons at all costs. Not only did he know based off the numerous voice mails and texts his boss had left for him over the past two days that the man was ultra pissed, David was also deeply disturbed by his boss's interaction with the white-haired man and his potential connection to Nick's death. But David had no choice but to chance it—he had to dig into the case involving the Upella Group and Zeitler. He'd called Leo, his paralegal, in advance to find out when Lyons was scheduled to be in a meeting and planned to sneak in and out of the office accordingly.

In hushed tones, Leo told him that Lyons was furious at him for not returning his calls or alerting him to his current whereabouts. The partner had come by Leo's office several times today, asking the paralegal if he'd heard *anything* from David. David explained to Leo that everything was fine—he had an important family matter he had to immediately address. He apologized if Leo had gotten caught in the cross fire in any way. Leo told him not to worry. Before hanging up, David asked if Leo had ever seen a guy in his thirties with short white hair around the office, possibly wearing a black jacket. Leo said he couldn't recall anyone like that. David asked Leo to let him know if he ever did.

Timing it just right, David walked into the firm's lobby and made a beeline down the hallway. He headed straight for the records room. He tried not to make eye contact with others, hoping to avoid any conversations that might delay his exit. Bolting into the records room, he found a clerk sitting at a cubicle with a dozen rows of shelves behind him loaded down with case files. Although he could have had Leo gather these items for him, David didn't want to put the paralegal's job in any jeopardy. Leo had a young family, and Lyons had proved to be ruthless with disloyal staff. Plus, David didn't want *anyone* at the firm even knowing about his private investigation into the Upella Group.

"Hey, David," said Andy, the red-haired clerk, "you need something?"

"No, just need to grab a few files myself."

"I could have brought them over to you."

"I know, but I'm in a hurry."

"All right."

The usual process for getting client material was through an online request. But David didn't want to check out anything officially. He moved past the clerk, scanned the rows, found the client number for the Upella Group. He pulled several accordion files off the shelf, quickly sorted through them, then grabbed the file for the litigation matter that Nick had been working on with Lyons when he died. David bolted for the door with the file tucked under his arm.

"Hey, David," Andy called out, "you need to check that out."

"Bringing it right back," David said, hitting the hallway before the clerk could say anything else about it.

David walked briskly down the hallway and into the lobby, where he punched the down button for the elevators and shifted his weight back and forth. He could feel sweat beading up on his back. Just when an elevator dinged, he heard an unhappy voice bark out his name from behind. Turning, he found the red face of Marty Lyons glaring at him.

David cursed under his breath. Lyons had probably asked staff to alert him if they spotted David.

"I need you in my office right now," Lyons demanded through clenched teeth.

The Upella Group file under his arm, David reluctantly followed his boss down the hallway. He thought of trying to dump the file somewhere en route to Lyons's office but couldn't find an opening without being too obvious.

Lyons shut his office door behind them, stomped over to his desk. David wasn't sure whether to stand or sit, so he just stood awkwardly in front of his boss's desk, the sweat on his back now a flowing river. He glanced at the file under his arm, made sure the Upella Group label was not openly showing. He tried to think of something to say if Lyons asked him directly about the file. He was drawing a blank. He couldn't help but take a quick peek over toward the floor-to-ceiling bookshelves along the left wall. The shelves were stuffed full of hundreds of thick legal books. Lyons basically had his own library. Although David couldn't immediately spot it, he knew there was a small hidden camera placed somewhere amid all those books. It was still so hard to imagine that Benny had actually planted the camera or even known how it all worked.

Lyons dropped into his chair, again glared at David. "Where the hell have you been?"

David swallowed. "Dealing with the death of a friend, sir. I'm sorry."

Lyons's eyes narrowed. "You couldn't at least call and give me notice?"

There were no condolences from the partner—no surprise. Lyons had proved to be a shallow man. But was he involved with the death of a lawyer?

David shifted his weight. "Again, I apologize, sir. I've had my phone off. The whole thing has had me pretty shaken up."

Lyons erupted. "Yet your grief didn't keep you from signing on to represent a low-life drug dealer who's being charged with murder."

David cocked his head. How did Lyons already know?

"The accused is no drug dealer," David tried to explain. "He's a good kid, and he's innocent."

"I don't give a rat's ass if he's innocent," Lyons countered. "We don't handle that kind of thing here at Hunter and Kellerman."

"I'd respectfully like to request an exception, sir. This is important to me."

"I don't give a damn!" Lyons barked. "The only thing that should be important to *you* is what's important to *me*. You'll drop this thing immediately, or else."

"Or else what?" David blurted out, irritated.

It was a foolish comment. He immediately regretted it. But he was on edge, considering the circumstances around Nick's death. He watched his boss closely, wondering if everything was about to unravel on him. To his credit, Lyons kept his cool. His boss took a deep breath, exhaled, stood, and circled around to the front of his desk, where he leaned against the edge. David pushed the file even farther under his armpit. He felt sweat on his forehead now.

"What are you doing, David? Are you trying to jeopardize your whole future?"

"It's difficult to explain, sir."

"Try me. Because you've worked too damn hard to get here to throw it all away now. Have we not showered you with praise and thrown gobs of money at you? Is this not everything you told me you wanted for your life? But now you want to jeopardize *everything* to represent a street kid who should probably be in jail anyway?"

Again, David wondered what Lyons knew. Could his boss know that the white-haired man had shot and killed Benny? David couldn't be sure—he had no real proof yet. So far, it was all just circumstantial. He needed to walk a fine line here.

"I just want to help someone whom I think is innocent, that's all."

"Fine. So help him by finding him another attorney. You barely have your bar license, son. There's no reason for you to stick your own neck out there *and* put unwanted attention on the firm by doing this. I need you to drop it today and get back to the real work of this firm. This is where you belong. Not out there dealing with this city's riffraff."

David knew that Lyons was probably right. Another criminal attorney could certainly handle the case better—even if he'd promised Larue he would. He thought of Benny, the hidden camera, the hired actor, the surveillance photos. Was it all real? Or had *everything* they'd found so far somehow been concocted in the mind of an unstable old man? There was still so much uncertainty behind the truth. David had to ask himself if he was truly ready to confront his boss about all this and potentially torpedo his whole future with Hunter & Kellerman.

"Do we understand each other, David?"

For the first time, Lyons's eyes drifted down to the file David was holding.

"Yes, sir, we do," David quickly answered. "I'll get back to work ASAP."

David spun, headed straight for the door.

THIRTY-THREE

David spent the next couple of hours camped in his office, pretending to work on his assigned caseload, just in case Lyons was keeping tabs on him. But he used most of that time secretly searching every nuance of the Upella Group and Zeitler litigation file. Again, nothing about the case stood out to him. It read like any standard case, with one company suing another over claims of misrepresentation. David was currently working on three other cases that looked almost exactly the same. The email communication in the file read just like normal everyday lawyer-speak. It wasn't even overly contentious. Just rich lawyers on both sides getting even richer off their clients while slowly working out the details of a litigation matter. So why had Benny printed out the news article about this case and highlighted the names of Nick and Lyons? Why did Nick tell Lyons in the text exchange that he wanted to go to the police? Where was the blackmail angle that Carla had said Nick mentioned to her before his death?

Frustrated, David finally sneaked out of the building and drove over to Jen's office. The *Advocate* operated out of a tiny ten-by-ten-foot office space beside an old pawnshop of crumbling bricks that sat along Twelfth Street—a block away from what Jen called Crack Alley. Jen had told David the paper had been started by a guy named Mickey Roose, a veteran of the newspaper industry who had spent forty-five years as a reporter and then as an editor. Mickey was now eighty-six and had trouble getting around. Although he came to the office once or twice a week, he'd handed the whole operation to Jen two years ago. Donations from the community barely covered Jen's meager living costs. Most writers and editors donated their time to help with the paper. A local printer offered its machines for free. Jen said it was a far cry from her life at the *Washington Post*, but she'd never felt more satisfied.

When the shock of what they'd found in Benny's belongings had worn off last night, Jen had switched into full-on investigative-reporter mode. She got busy digging deeper into everything from Benny's bag to see if she could start putting some pieces together. She said she still had good sources and contacts from her days in Washington. After leaving the encounter with his boss, David almost hoped Jen had found *something* that verified that Benny was simply a crazy man who was prone to dreaming up wild conspiracies. In some ways, David wanted to put this whole ordeal behind him and get on with his regularly scheduled life. However, he couldn't stop thinking about Larue, Doc, Shifty, Curly, and the other boys at the Camp. Doc had said he belonged with them. That had meant a lot to David. Then again, Lyons said he belonged at Hunter & Kellerman.

David felt caught in the sudden tension of two polar-opposite worlds.

Jen was at a small wooden desk with a computer that was crammed into one corner of the tiny room. A folding table next to her was covered with stacks of old newspapers that nearly touched the stained ceiling tiles. A wooden shelf was loaded down with old journalism books. The only window to the outside in the room had protective bars over it. Jen said she'd watched countless drug deals going down on the sidewalk right in front of her.

"You find anything in the file?" Jen asked him.

"Nothing," David responded. "What about you?"

Jen handed David a printout of what looked like an official navy profile. "Benjamin Edward Dugan. I ran the photo of him and the other sailors by an old military source. Benny served from 1970 to 1978, including a stint in Atsugi, Japan, as the photo suggests."

David stared at the face of the sailor on the printout—the wrinkle-free young face of Benny. He'd recognize those eyes anywhere. He scanned farther down the profile page on Benny and came across more intriguing info.

"Benny was an intelligence specialist?" David asked.

Jen nodded. "Office of Naval Intelligence. Benny was part of the Naval Reconnaissance and Technical Support Center."

"So he really did know what he was doing with all of this gear?"

"Yes, that appears to be the case," Jen agreed. "I also searched for any mention of Benjamin Edward Dugan over the past ten years. There is literally *nothing* out there about him. Benny completely fell off the online map a decade ago and has never resurfaced."

"What about his family?"

"I'm pretty sure I've found Benny's daughter," Jen confirmed, handing him another printout. "I cross-referenced Benny's full name with the name *Cassie Ray* that we found written on the back of the photo of the woman holding the baby. There was a birth announcement in a local paper outside of Memphis about ten years ago. Benjamin Dugan was listed as the grandfather. Which, of course, would make the woman in the photo his daughter. Her name is Jessica Bowman. I have her contact information. She's still living near Memphis. Divorced. A fourth-grade teacher, it appears. I haven't done anything with it yet. I thought you might want to personally make that call to Jessica."

"I do, thanks."

Jen kept doling out new information. "I also contacted both Austin Camera and Imaging and the Austin Spy Shop. The guy at the camera place has no recollection of someone matching Benny's description purchasing a Nikon camera, but he's only there part-time. He agreed to ask his boss about it. I'm supposed to call back later. However, the guy who runs the Austin Spy Shop clearly remembers Benny coming in and buying the surveillance kit. He was surprised that a guy like Benny—probably meaning someone that old who looked and dressed like Benny—seemed to really know his way around some of the gear. But that's not even the most interesting thing I found."

"What is?"

"I contacted the taxi service that Benny used that one day. They were able to tell me the locations of the drop-off and pickup connected to those substantial charges."

"How'd you get them to do that?"

"Said I was doing an investigative piece on taxi-company scams. They became more than eager to help me and verify they were legitimate."

"I'll bet. So where did Benny go?"

"A medical care facility outside San Antonio called Harbor Courts. It's primarily a center for residents suffering from severe dementia."

David pondered that reveal. "Wonder who Benny went there to see?"

Jen shrugged. "That's as far as I've gotten."

"Let's go find out."

THIRTY-FOUR

They immediately jumped into his Range Rover and headed south on I-35. The navigation system said they could be at the medical facility within an hour and a half. David put a heavy foot on the gas pedal. He decided to keep his earlier conversation with Lyons private from Jen for now. Larue's arraignment with the judge was scheduled for nine the following morning. The way David figured, he still had about nineteen hours to sort through all this before he faced an agonizing decision. He grimaced at the prospect of telling Jen and the boys at the Camp that he could no longer represent Larue.

Speeding down the highway, with Jen continuing to do research on her cell phone, David thought about Benny's visit to this facility. Someone crucial to the situation had to be living there. The old man wouldn't have spent $500 on cab rides for no good reason. David could feel the anticipation building. What was behind all this? The old man had orchestrated a dangerous back-alley encounter with David, using a hired muscle-bound actor, and had allowed himself to take a serious physical blow—one that could have put Benny in the hospital for good with permanent brain damage. Why would Benny put himself at such risk? The old man had clearly chosen David in advance in an effort to somehow get access to monitor Marty Lyons. Why?

On the drive, David made the difficult phone call to Jessica Bowman, Benny's estranged daughter. He had no idea if Benny had been in contact with her, so it felt awkward to call her up out of the blue and explain that her father was now dead—killed in cold blood. The call went straight to voice mail. Rather than explaining anything in his message, David simply identified himself, said the call was about a man named Benjamin Dugan, and asked her to please call him back.

Harbor Courts was an exquisite, one-story redbrick building in an affluent neighborhood of parks, trails, and lush greenery. They parked in a visitor spot out front and entered the main lobby. A well-decorated sitting area was to the left. David walked up to the front desk, where they were greeted by a woman with brown hair with a name tag that said Rebecca.

She looked up, smiled appropriately. "Can I help you?"

"I sure hope so," David replied. He dropped his attorney business card. "My name's David Adams, and this is my associate, Jen Cantwell. I'm an attorney representing the estate of a man named Benjamin Dugan. Mr. Dugan visited your facility a few weeks back." David showed her the photo of Benny he had on his phone. "We need to verify whom this man came here to see on that day."

Rebecca looked uneasy. "Oh, okay. Well, I'm not really sure how to handle that. We have very strict privacy policies here."

"This is a very important legal matter, Rebecca," David pressed.

"I understand that . . . it's just . . . let me get our director to speak with you."

Rebecca stood, then disappeared down a hallway. David and Jen shared a look. Would this work? Standing there, David noticed a young black woman in her twenties behind the front counter, filing paperwork in cabinets. She'd been watching their conversation closely. Two minutes later, a stern-faced fiftysomething woman wearing a black suit walked in front of the check-in counter and stood face-to-face with them. She did not have the look of a woman who was easily intimidated. She looked like a bulldog in a suit. She offered a hand to them both, introduced herself as Jackie, director of Harbor Courts.

"What can I do for you, Mr. Adams?" she asked.

"As I explained to Rebecca, I need to verify whom my client visited while he was here with you a few weeks ago. I have the exact date, if that's helpful."

"I'm afraid we can't give you that information without a court order. It goes directly against the confidentiality agreements we have in place with our residents and their families. I'm very sorry I can't help you."

David stood his ground. They could not leave without finding out whom Benny saw. "Look, Jackie, I appreciate your confidentiality, I do. I certainly understand the need for it legally. But I also need you to understand something." He again held up the photo of Benny on his phone. "This man, my client, was killed in cold blood two nights ago. Violently gunned down in an alley. Police are investigating. It's a big mess. We think there could be a connection here. I'm trying to save you the trouble of being pulled into the middle of all of it."

David peeked over, again spotted the young woman monitoring their heated conversation. When she noticed his glance, she quickly looked away.

The bulldog didn't budge an inch. "My deepest condolences about your client. That's horrible to hear. But it unfortunately doesn't change our stance on confidentiality. We simply can't make exceptions for any-one outside of a court order."

Frustrated, David and Jen walked slowly back to the parking lot. After getting into his car, David watched as the young woman who'd been filing paperwork briskly made her way from the front doors of Harbor Courts and ran over to his Range Rover. David rolled down his window as she approached.

"Can I see the photo?" she asked David. Her name tag said Kim.

He pulled up the photo of Benny, showed it to her. She took a good, hard look at it.

"Was he really murdered?" she asked, looking across to Jen, who nodded.

"Two days ago," Jen confirmed.

Kim covered her mouth, eyes still on the photo. "That's so tragic."

"Do you recognize him?" David asked.

"Yes, I remember him well," Kim replied. "He was so sweet. I was having a really bad day, and he was kind enough to ask me if I was okay. I don't usually talk about my life with strangers, but this man just had an inviting way about him. I told him that my car had broken down a week prior, and I was exhausting myself while having to take my two children on a city bus every morning and afternoon, all the way across town, to get to their school. Both of my kids go to a special school to help them with learning issues. The travel time had put an incredible strain on us, but I didn't have the money to get my car fixed—everything I had was going to pay for this school. Right on the spot, this nice old man pulled four hundred dollars out of his pocket and gave it to me. And he didn't ask for anything in return. I couldn't believe it."

David smiled. "That sounds like Benny."

"He didn't sign in as Benny," Kim said, confused. "He used a different name, although I can't recall it at the moment."

"Do you know who he was here to see?" Jen asked.

Kim nodded, shifted awkwardly. "He came to see Jerry. He had this little video camera with him, said he was putting something together for a reunion with former navy buddies. He spent several hours in Jerry's room. I peeked in a few times. Jerry never says much to anyone. He mostly just sits in his room all day, staring blankly out the window, completely disoriented. But I could tell something clicked for Jerry that day when this nice old man was with him. It was like the fog briefly cleared, which sometimes happens when our residents have visitors from their pasts. For a brief moment, you get to see who they were before they came to us."

David glanced over at Jen. A video camera?

"What is Jerry's last name?" he asked Kim.

"Landon. Jerry Landon."

David noticed Jen jotting the name down on a small notepad. He decided to ask for something bolder. "Kim, can you get us in to see Jerry?"

Another uneasy shift of weight. Then she nodded. "Okay. That man, Benny, was an absolute angel to me that day." She pointed over toward the side of the building. "Take the sidewalk through the gate. Jerry is all the way in the back. Meet me by the outside doors to the reflection gardens in a few minutes."

Kim rushed back inside. They waited.

"They must have served together," David said to Jen.

Jen nodded. "Jerry is one of the names on the back of Benny's photo."

After a few minutes, they got out and circled around the side of the building, where they found a lush garden area. Several residents were out walking in the gardens. A few were in wheelchairs accompanied by what looked like family members. David and Jen approached the facility door that led to the gardens. Kim was ready for them. She opened the door, quickly ushered them inside. They followed her down a hallway, turned a corner, and stopped in front of a door to a resident's room. David looked through a small window, where he saw an old man sitting in a chair by a curtained window. A bed set was on one side of the spacious room, a sofa and two chairs on the other. The room was warm and well decorated.

"Please be quick," Kim begged them. "I don't want to lose my job."

"We will, I promise," Jen reassured her. "Will he talk to us?"

Kim shrugged. "Like I said, he never says a word. But he did with Benny. I'll wait here until you're finished."

David and Jen opened the bedroom door, entered Jerry's room. The old man never turned to look or even acknowledge their presence. David approached him cautiously, entering the man's line of sight. Jerry wore brown slacks, black slippers, and a gray cardigan. He looked frail beneath the clothes. Yet he still had a thick head of silver hair.

"Hi, Jerry, my name's David. This is Jen."

Jerry never moved. His eyes remained locked on the window.

"We're friends with Benny," Jen added.

Again, no response from Jerry. Not even an eye flinch.

Jen knelt in front of the man, using her warmest voice. "Do you remember Benny Dugan? Benny from the navy?"

Jerry took a slow glance at Jen but again didn't say anything. While Jen continued to try to gently pull Jerry out of the fog somehow, David wandered over to a set of bookshelves in the room. They were filled with framed photos of what looked like different grandkids of various ages. A more upright and alert Jerry was in the middle of several of them, looking like a much different man than he was right now. On one shelf, David found a framed picture of a young Jerry wearing his navy uniform. Right next to it, he found the exact same group photo that Benny had in his possession. Seven men all standing together on a dock somewhere. Benny was the first guy on the left. From comparing the solo photo of Jerry in uniform, David noted that he was the second guy from the right. They had indeed served together. Opening the frame, David pulled the photo out. There was nothing written on the back.

"Jen?" David said, showing her the photo.

She walked over, took a look. "Maybe we can track down some of the other guys in the photo. See if they can tell us anything."

"If Benny took a video of Jerry, where is it?" David asked. "We have all of his things."

Jen shrugged. "And, more important, what's on it?"

David looked back over at the frail old man. "No luck, huh?"

She shook her head. "It's really sad."

"Okay, come on," David said. "Let's not get Kim into trouble."

"Wait," Jen said, grabbing another framed photo from the bookshelf. In the photo, a healthy version of Jerry stood by a younger man, probably in his late thirties, who shared his likeness. Behind them was a building with *Upella Group* plastered on the front. "Jerry is connected to the Upella Group?"

"Joe Landon," David said, suddenly putting two and two together. "He's the founder and CEO of the Upella Group. Jerry must be his father."

"Do you know anything about Joe Landon?"

David shook his head. "Only what I just told you."

Jen was already on her phone again, searching Google. She found quick results. "Well, by this time next year, Joe Landon could be a household name."

"Why?"

"He's running for Congress in Texas's Thirty-Second Congressional District."

"Seriously?"

"Yes, he's one of the guys battling it out for the chance to oust the incumbent next fall. Landon's got a good pedigree, too." Jen was searching and reporting her findings. "He served in Iraq as an army Ranger, where it's been widely reported that he saved the lives of two men from his battalion during a hostile operation. The Upella Group is now worth over four hundred million dollars. One report claims Landon has already spent ten million dollars of his own money on the campaign, and insiders say he's willing to spend three times that, if necessary, to win. The spending is working. Early polls are showing Landon already running neck and neck when matched up with the incumbent and gaining momentum. Most from his party view him as a future superstar who could make a run at the White House one day."

David was trying to piece things together. "Maybe this wasn't about a litigation matter. Maybe this was about a man."

"You think Benny had something on Jerry and chose to use it against Joe Landon?"

"I think I might have gotten pulled into the middle of two desperate men. One desperate to help his friends. Another desperate to protect his power."

"We have to find that video, David."

THIRTY-FIVE

Frank Hodges knocked on the hotel suite door, which seemed to be his client's preferred meeting place. Although it was only late afternoon, his client's eyes were already completely bloodshot. He also reeked of alcohol. *This should be fun,* Frank thought. He followed his client into the suite. His client went straight to the bar, refilled his glass, and then dropped heavily into a chair in the living room. There was an air of desperation to him. Frank knew desperate people did really stupid things. He took a position across the coffee table from the man.

Reaching down, his client slid him a folder.

Frank opened it, found a list of names on top. "What is this?"

"More possible loose ends. I need to know what these people know ASAP."

"There are twelve names on this list."

"Correct."

"And how do you figure we go about doing that?" Frank asked.

"Hell if I know!" his client blurted out. "You're the expert. Tap all of their phones, hack their emails, follow them, interrogate them, waterboard them. Figure it the hell out."

"What exactly would we be looking for?"

"It's summarized in the file."

Frank sighed, put the file down. "If we find out someone on this list does know something that you don't want shared, then what?"

"You let me worry about that."

"When does it stop?"

"When my clients say to stop! We have a serious problem here, Hodges! A problem we both need to deal with right now before this blows up in all of our faces."

Frank was not at all happy with the way his client kept saying *we* in his paranoid references. Frank was not one of *them*. He'd done what he was hired to do, and had gone above and beyond to help track down Benjamin Dugan. Something he was now seriously regretting. Out of his own curiosity, Frank had gone back to the surveillance video of the original money drop and had found Dugan sitting in the sixth row of the church, hunched down while dressed in a trench coat and a knit cap. The old man had somehow lifted the *X* envelope himself. Dugan had been so smooth with the velvet bag that Frank still couldn't see it, even while enhancing the video.

"I'm afraid my job here is done," Frank explained. "We're pulling out today."

His client glared at Frank. "What? You can't leave now."

Frank remained calm. "I assure you, I can. And I will."

The man bolted out of his chair, cursing loudly. "This isn't finished, Hodges! We need your help. What should've been a simple job has turned into a total disaster. There are too many loose ends on this thing and too many people for us to track by ourselves. We need your team in place *right now* to finish this damn job, or we're all going to prison."

Frank knew exactly what *finishing the job* meant to his client. How many people were they willing to kill? While Frank was okay living in the murky gray area that it took to operate in the dark world of private security, he also had his limits.

He stood. "This is your mess, not mine."

"Please!" his client begged. "Just name your price, Hodges. I can get you whatever you need. My client will spend whatever it takes to promptly resolve this matter. He's worth hundreds of millions of dollars. But you can't walk out on us right now. He'll never allow it."

Frank cocked his head. "Is that a threat?"

"It's the truth. I promise you, if he goes down, we all go down."

"Best of luck to you."

As Frank walked to the door, he heard his client yell another string of expletives, make more drunken threats, and then toss his glass of bourbon across the room. Frank never flinched. He'd once stood in front of a terrorist leader in Egypt who put a sword to his neck. He'd escaped a Russian execution squad while on assignment in Saint Petersburg. He'd sidestepped a sniper attack in Tel Aviv. Men like this didn't scare him in the least.

But his client was correct about one thing.

There were loose ends.

THIRTY-SIX

They huddled back inside Jen's office. Night was upon the city. There was a new energy to their pursuit—David knew they were *really* close to finally finding the truth. Benny had clearly put an intricate plan in action against a powerful and sinister player, and that had ultimately cost him his life. Benny had something *big*—David felt sure of that. But what, exactly? What was at the center of the old man's plan? What could Benny have had that would scare someone into killing him? Jerry, the old man at the facility, probably knew but wouldn't (or couldn't) talk to them. Outside of finding the video, their only other hope was that another member from the navy photo knew the same thing as Jerry and *would* talk to them.

Jen had again reached out to her military source on the drive back from San Antonio in an effort to identify each man in the photo. As they waited, Jen continued to research everything she could possibly find on Joe Landon, trying to find *any* angle that might help lead them to the truth. Behind her, David paced in a tight circle around the small office, racking his brain, and making himself dizzy. Marty Lyons had started incessantly calling him again—and David kept hitting "Ignore." He knew the fuse had again been lit.

In one way or another, this was all about to blow up on him.

Jen read from her computer screen. "Landon received the Silver Star for his lifesaving actions back in Iraq. Several years ago, a reporter from the *Dallas Morning News* wrote up a detailed account of the event. It reads like an action-movie script. Landon's got American hero written all over him. Apparently, he risked his own life to pull two men out of a burning Jeep that was under heavy enemy fire and dragged them more than fifty yards to safety."

David considered that. "We all have a dark side. Power can make a man crazy."

Jen suddenly gasped, startling him. "Look at this!"

He quickly leaned over her shoulder. Jen was pointing at a photograph from the *Dallas Morning News* article of a young Landon wearing his military fatigues, leaning up against a Jeep in Iraq, with several other soldiers hanging around him. Two of the soldiers in the photo were highlighted as the men he'd saved. Jen placed her finger an inch from the screen, aimed directly at the face of one of the young soldiers.

"Is that him?" Jen asked. "Is that the white-haired man from Benny's photos?"

David's eyes widened. "Yes, that's definitely him. That's the same guy I saw outside Nick's house, in his office two days later, and meeting with my boss outside the airplane. That's probably the same guy who killed Benny."

"His name is Mark Appleton. From Claremore, Oklahoma."

David cursed. "So Landon saves this guy's neck back in Iraq, and now he calls him in to return the favor?"

"Maybe Larue can identify this guy?"

"I had planned to show him the surveillance photos tomorrow."

Jen noticed an email arrive in her in-box. It was from her military source, who had done quick work in identifying the other navy men in the photo with Benny and Jerry. Jen now had a full list of names, two of which were already marked as deceased. Family members had filed official paperwork with the military a long time ago. They focused on the three remaining guys on the list. Jen began a quick Google search of their full names. David returned to his pacing behind her. Everything Larue had told him about that fateful night in the alley with Benny was legit. Mark Appleton was a highly trained soldier, and he owed Joe Landon his life. It was no longer far-fetched that he might use a gun with a silencer to take down Benny. Appleton also had been at Benny's burial service. Why? Who was he watching?

Looking down at Jen, David felt uneasy. He'd pulled her right into this dangerous deal.

"Take a look at this," Jen said, eyes on her screen.

David looked in from behind again. "What is it?"

"The obituaries from the *Casper Star-Tribune* a month ago. Sammy Diermont, the third guy from the right in the photo, just died in a hiking accident."

"Check the others, Jen."

Jen typed in another name from the group, immediately found an easy hit. "What the hell, David?"

David read the computer screen—a blurb from the *Journal-Spectator*, a small newspaper out of Wharton, Texas. Charles Hicks died of an apparent suicide, gunshot to the head. No foul play suspected.

Jen typed in the last name on the list. Another immediate hit—and yet *another* reported death. Marvin Shobert had died in an apparent mugging at a horse track near Dallas.

"All from the same week," David said, feeling the air knocked out of him.

"*Every* one of them is dead."

"Except for Jerry Landon."

"We have to go to the police, David. Right now. People are dying all over the place because of this. I know one of the detectives. He's done a lot of volunteer work with us. We can go straight to him and give him everything. I trust him."

"Okay, but let's at least go back out to the Camp one last time and search for the video, just to see if Benny might have found a spot to hide it out there. Without the video, it still feels like a lot of speculation on our part."

"Okay, I'll go with you."

Exiting the building, David and Jen hurried into the small parking lot and climbed into David's SUV. Jen realized she'd forgotten her phone and rushed back inside the building. David glanced across the street while waiting and suddenly noticed someone standing beside a car near a streetlight, staring directly over at him. It sent a shiver of fear straight up his back.

Mark Appleton.

Cursing, David jumped out of his car to go grab Jen. A sudden explosion behind him shattered the pawnshop's front windows and knocked David forward, where he slammed his face up against the brick of the building. For a second, he couldn't hear a thing, just a ringing in his ears. His vision was also blurry. And it felt like his lungs were on fire. Lying facedown on the pavement, he turned over, trying to figure out what had just happened. There was a ball of fire in the parking lot behind him, billows of smoke filling the air. Then he suddenly recognized that his Range Rover was in the middle of the fire, being completely swallowed in flames.

David's head pounded. He could barely focus. He looked down, noticed that his pants were on fire. He quickly patted them down with his bare hands, putting out the small flames. His palms were completely covered in black. His skin was stinging. What the hell had just happened?

He suddenly felt hands under his arms, pulling on him. He looked up, found Jen trying to drag him away from the scorching fire. Two other cars in the small parking lot were also engulfed in flames. In his first moment of clarity, David remembered Appleton standing across the street. Pushing himself up onto wobbly feet, David spun around to look in that direction, but he couldn't see anything through all the smoke and flames.

David grabbed Jen by the hand and ran like hell.

THIRTY-SEVEN

Sitting behind the wheel of Jen's Ford Escape, which had been parked on the opposite side of the pawnshop, David drove like a madman through the streets of East Austin, the tires squealing at every sharp turn. Although his ears still had a faint ringing, his hearing had gradually returned, and his vision had cleared. But he still felt a stinging in his fingers.

Jen sat next to him, holding on tightly to the handle by the passenger door, looking freaked out of her mind. She had taken a white T-shirt from her back seat and was trying her best to clean David's charred face while he tossed her all about with his reckless driving. The white T-shirt was now completely covered in black.

"You're bleeding badly," she said, shaking her head. "We need to take you to the hospital. You could have internal injuries."

"I will, but not yet."

She sat back, still holding on tight. "Are you sure you saw the guy?"

"Yes. And I'm sure that was a car bomb intended to kill us."

"This is crazy! What kind of person would do all of this?"

David thought of Lyons. Did his boss know about this? Nick's death clearly had not been a suicide. Could his boss have had Nick killed? Could Lyons have even given the okay to have his star protégé blown into a million pieces just now in order to protect his own client?

Speeding down the neighborhood street that led to the edge of the woods, David immediately noticed something different up ahead. He cursed, pulled the car to the curb. A huge orange ball of fire was licking the night sky in front of them. Three fire trucks and several police cars were already stationed at the very edge of the street, where David had parked his Range Rover to take the path into the woods. A crowd had gathered to watch, as it looked like the entire forest was engulfed in flames.

"David!" Jen said, eyes locked on the fire trucks. "The Camp?"

David felt a thick ball of fear develop in his stomach. The boys! They both jumped out of the car and sprinted forward toward the big crowd.

"Shep!" someone called out in the chaos.

David turned, spotted Doc and then Curly, Elvis, and Shifty, all standing at the edge of the crowd. He immediately felt a rush of relief. They were okay. But what about the other guys? The boys hurried over to him. He could see the shock in the men's faces.

"What happened, Doc?" David asked.

Doc just shook his head. "A man showed up about an hour ago, waving a gun around, scaring the hell out of all of us. He had a big gas container with him. He started shooting in the air, running us all off, and then he began pouring gas over *everything*. He set it all on fire. He burned down the Camp, Shep!"

David cursed. "White-haired guy?"

"Yeah," Doc replied, forehead bunched. "How'd you know that?"

David cursed again. The panic button had been pressed. They'd probably burned down the camp just in case there was evidence out there—like the video. No one was safe anymore.

"I'll explain later," David said. "Did everyone get out okay?"

"I don't know," Doc said. "I think so. We tried our best to scramble, to make sure everyone got out, but I can't be sure yet. The fire grew so quickly. We all had to just run for it."

"What do we do?" Shifty asked, looking dazed, confused. "He burned down our homes. We have nothing and nowhere to go."

"Don't worry," David said. "I'll take care of you. All of you."

THIRTY-EIGHT

On the way to the police station, David felt his cell phone buzz. He pulled it out of his pocket and recognized the number from the phone call he'd placed to Memphis earlier that afternoon.

"Who is it?" Jen asked.

"Jessica Bowman. Benny's daughter."

"You should take it. She needs to know."

David pulled over to a curb two blocks from police headquarters, answered on speakerphone. He tried to sound calm, although his voice felt shaky. "Jessica, this is David Adams. Thank you for returning my phone call."

"You said this was about Benjamin Dugan."

"Benjamin was your father?"

"Yes." A long pause. "Is he dead?"

David was surprised by such a straightforward question. Jessica had also asked it without much emotion behind it. There was no way for him to sugarcoat his answer. He just had to tell her the truth.

"Yes, I'm afraid your father passed away two days ago. We were only able to find you today. I'm very sorry for your loss."

Jessica sighed. "I've been expecting this call for many years now, to be honest. My father chose his way of life a long time ago. I knew it would eventually lead to this one day. You're actually saving *me* a phone call, Mr. Adams."

David and Jen shared a curious look. "How's that?"

"I received a letter from my father out of the blue a few days ago. He made many apologies about his decade-long absence, especially because he's never even met his only grandchild. My father's letter was brief. He was never much for words. He didn't ask me for anything. But he told me, should I ever find out that something had happened to him, I should call a lawyer named David Adams. He gave me your phone number. He also wrote down an address at the bottom of the letter, along with some kind of number combination, and he said I should give you the info when I called you."

David and Jen shared a look. He felt his adrenaline spike again. He asked Jessica to read him the address, which she did, while Jen scribbled it all down on a piece of paper. Jen then immediately began typing the address into her phone.

"Is that all that was in the letter, Jessica?" David asked.

"No, my father also mentioned that he'd left some money for me and Cassie Ray. He said you'd send it to me." She sighed again. "I'm not expecting much of anything."

"If I find something, I'll definitely send it to you. I promise."

"Okay, thank you."

David felt a deep sadness settle on him. This was Benny's daughter. His only family. "Jessica, you need to know that your father was a special friend to me. As a matter of fact, he was special to *a lot* of people here in Austin."

She was quiet for a moment. "Did he suffer?"

"No, he passed away instantly." David didn't feel it necessary to expound on the wild story behind Benny's death. Jessica had suffered enough already.

"I've got to go," Jessica said.

"Okay, but keep my number. If you or Cassie ever need *anything*, please don't hesitate to call me. I want to help you any way I can."

She thanked him and hung up.

David looked over at Jen. She held up her phone to show him a map on her screen.

"Where is it?" David asked.

"Austin Bike Tours and Rentals. Four blocks from here."

"Let's go."

David did a quick U-turn, spun the tires.

David pulled the car to a stop in front of a huge light-blue shipping container that had been converted into a makeshift bike shop with a sign above it that said Austin Bike Tours and Rentals. It was late—the bike shop was currently closed. Just the same, David and Jen got out, walked up to it, the note with the number combination in Jen's hands.

"The lockers," Jen said, veering around to the side of the container.

At the end of the shipping container, they found a wall of built-in small metal lockers where bikers stored small amounts of gear during rides. The lockers were labeled from one to two hundred. The address Jessica had passed along to them said #82. David found the locker on the bottom row. Like dozens of others, it currently had a combination lock on it. What was inside? The video? His heart raced. Jen read out the combination as David spun the lock back and forth in his fingers until the lock released. Tugging open the locker door, he found a small black banker bag inside. David quickly unzipped the bag and took a peek. Not only did he find the *X* envelope Benny had on him the first night they'd met, still filled with a load of cash, but David also discovered a handheld Flip video camera. David looked up at Jen, both of them feeling the energy of the moment.

They rushed back over to Jen's car and dropped inside. Turning on the ceiling light, David quickly skimmed the cash in the envelope. Benny still had thousands of dollars left. He'd make sure to get that to Jessica. David examined the handheld camera. It had a port that popped out to download captured videos easily onto computers or external drives. But did the camera still have a video loaded on it? He pressed the camera's red circular button and watched the small digital screen come to life.

He found only one video—a screen capture of Jerry Landon's now-familiar face. David pressed "Play" as they watched in silence.

THIRTY-NINE

On the video, Jerry Landon sat in the same chair by the window where they'd tried to engage with him a few hours earlier. However, he looked much different. His eyes were focused and alert; there was even a bit more color in the old man's face. He seemed lucid, like he was another person. As Kim had mentioned to them, Benny's visit had somehow momentarily snapped Jerry back to reality. In his hands, Jerry held the framed navy group photo, as if the two men had been reminiscing about old times. The recording started when the two old men appeared to be deep into their visit together. Jerry seemed at ease sitting there with Benny. However, David noted that it didn't seem like Jerry was even aware their conversation was being recorded, as if Benny were discreetly holding the camera in his lap. The video showed only Jerry in the shot.

"You remember that night?" Benny asked, off camera.

Jerry, who had been smiling, suddenly frowned. "It's haunted me my whole life."

"I think it's haunted all of us," Benny added.

"Should've never happened," Jerry said, shifting his frail weight in the chair.

"We were young and stupid. But Cliff *always* blamed you."

This made Jerry sit upright. "To hell with Cliff! *He* was the instigator. Not me."

"How do you remember it, Jerry?"

Jerry looked off, took a long moment. "It was Cliff's birthday, remember?" he said, turning back to Benny. "We hit the bars hard that night. We were all drunk as hell. More than usual. Marv took a swing at that big jarhead, and all hell broke loose. They kicked us out of that joint fast. We were all pretty worked up on the walk back to the barracks. That's when Cliff spotted her—the Asian girl. Cliff tried to be smooth, but he was a blabbering idiot. That girl didn't want any part of him; she just kept walking away. We all had a good laugh at his expense, which made Cliff really angry. He was always a hothead. Hell, he's the one who snapped that night! Not me! Cliff's the one who grabbed that girl and pulled her into the alley . . ."

Jerry swallowed, looked over toward the window again. A long moment passed.

"You take a turn?" Benny asked Jerry.

"Of course." He looked back at Benny. "Didn't you?"

"No, but I didn't stop it, either. She couldn't have been more than fourteen. I'll never stop hearing her screams. I never said a word about it to anyone."

"We had a pact," Jerry mentioned. "I suppose everyone kept it all these years."

"I suppose. We all deserve hell."

"Probably."

The video kept rolling as both men sat there in uncomfortable silence.

Jerry then turned to Benny again and angrily muttered, "Can't believe Cliff is trying to put that on me. If I ever see that fool again, I swear he's going to get a piece of me."

The video screen went black.

David looked over at Jen, who sat there wide-eyed. "Benny clearly went to Harbor Courts to talk to Jerry and try to get this story on camera. He must've used it to email Nick and Lyons after discovering they were Joe Landon's attorneys and tried to blackmail Landon. Having a father connected to something like this would certainly hurt Landon's campaign. And you told me he's already spent ten million dollars."

Jen nodded. "Landon might not survive the all-out media spectacle."

"So he tried to stop it. Enter Mark Appleton."

They were quickly putting the pieces together.

Jen shook her head. "Landon knew from the video that it originated from one of his father's old navy friends. He just didn't know which one."

"So he killed them all."

"Oh, Benny." Jen sighed. "What did you do?"

"Benny couldn't have anticipated this kind of escalating result. He completely misjudged how far Landon would go to cover this thing up. He got himself killed because of that, and he nearly got us and the rest of the boys killed, too."

"How wrapped up do you think your boss is in all of this?"

"I have my suspicions. But I need to confirm them."

"What are you going to do, David?"

He started the car, punched the gas pedal.

"I'm going to get the truth."

FORTY

David stood outside Lyons's office door, took a deep breath, and tried to gather himself. His heart was pounding. He could feel the weight of the moment. Six weeks ago, he'd walked into this building with stars in his eyes, dead set on impressing the hell out of the man who occupied this corner office, destroying his rookie rival in the process, and making mountains of cash for the rest of his life. Tonight, he entered the building ready to take his boss down in a blaze of glory.

To do that, he needed to confront Lyons face-to-face and somehow pull the truth out of him. David's gut said his boss's fingerprints were all over this deal. But Lyons was a savvy lawyer and still capable of sidestepping prosecution. David needed confirmation that Lyons was directly involved in Nick's death. Otherwise, Lyons might still get away with it.

David put his hand on the door handle, stepped fully into the office. Lyons was standing over by the huge windows, looking completely strung out and on the phone. The man's tie hung loose, and his hair was disheveled. One shirtsleeve was rolled up to the elbow, the other completely unraveled. He held a glass of brown liquid in his left hand, his phone pressed to his ear in his right hand.

Spotting David, Lyons immediately hung up without another word.

"What are you doing here?" Lyons asked, wide-eyed.

"You've been calling me incessantly, demanding I get back to the office ASAP."

His eyes narrowed. "Who knows you're here?"

"Why does that matter?"

"It doesn't . . . I'm just—"

"Surprised I survived the car bomb?"

David wanted to strike first, try to push his boss off-balance. He needed to be aggressive. Lyons would not like his protégé challenging him.

Lyons's forehead bunched. "Are you playing games with me, David?"

"This isn't a game, believe me. I have dead friends. I have burns all over my body."

"Don't blame me for that, son."

"Then who's to blame, Marty? Joe Landon?"

Another punch. David stepped farther into the office, inching closer to Lyons.

Lyons tilted his head, as if trying to figure out just how much David knew about everything. "What do you know about Joe Landon?"

"I know that the man so desperately wants to win a congressional seat that he sent out his old army buddy Mark Appleton to ensure that *nothing* stopped it from happening."

"I have no idea what you're talking about," Lyons insisted.

"Are *you* playing games with *me* now?" David asked. "I saw Appleton outside Nick's house that night. Just like I saw him rummaging through Nick's office two nights later and then meeting with you on the tarmac outside our plane that day. Hell, I have pictures of you two together, Marty. Nick's girlfriend told me about the blackmail email you received. I have the actual video of Landon's father in my possession. I know Nick wanted to go to the police. But you couldn't allow that to happen, could you?"

Lyons cursed, stepped over to his wet bar, refilled his glass. "I tried to protect Nick. Believe me, I exhausted myself. But he wouldn't listen. Just like I've been trying to protect you."

"Protect me from what?"

"From yourself, you idiot," Lyons said, tossing back his drink.

"Is that why you sent Melissa Masters to keep tabs on me? To protect me?"

"Of course! You should be grateful. I knew you saw something you shouldn't have seen. It's why I've been repeatedly trying to pull you back into the fold before it was too late. I've only been doing what you asked me to do from the very first time we met—get you to where I am. So don't stand there acting so self-righteous, son. You have no idea what all it has taken for me to build alliances with powerful people. I've only been trying to protect you and your future."

"And when I wouldn't listen, I had to die, too? Just like Nick?"

"Yes," Lyons said matter-of-factly. But he measured his next words. "However, you're still standing here. So, unlike with Nick, it's not too late for you. I can still protect you, David. But you have to make that commitment to me right now."

"Why, Marty? Why go through with all of this?"

"Joe Landon will be in the White House one day."

"Even if people have to die to get him there?"

"Don't be naive. People have had to die for decades to help candidates secure the White House. Can you imagine what that kind of power will do for us? We'll be rich beyond our dreams. We'll live like kings."

"But you're already unimaginably rich."

"Nonsense. This is pennies compared to where we're going. You can still come with me, son. Just say yes. All of this can be but a blip on the road map toward your glorious future."

David felt like he'd just gotten an invitation to hand his soul over to the devil himself.

"Benjamin Dugan's death is no blip. Neither is Nick's."

Lyons slowly frowned. "I can't protect you if you walk out that door again."

David glanced over toward the bookshelves, where he knew the secret surveillance camera Benny had installed was currently piping a live video feed to Jen's detective friend in an unmarked vehicle somewhere outside the building. Jen had taken the equipment, along with all the other evidence they'd gathered, over to police headquarters.

"I don't want your protection," David said. "You're going to prison."

As he left the office, Lyons cursed after him.

"You won't last a day, you fool!"

FORTY-ONE

Stepping out of the elevator into the lobby of the building, David breathed a huge sigh of relief. He'd accomplished what he'd needed. He'd gotten Lyons to own his involvement in Nick's death. But his relief was stolen away by the sudden appearance of Mark Appleton right in front of him. David panicked. The white-haired killer raised a gun in his hand, pointed it straight at David's head. A few other people who were also in the lobby noticed the armed man and started screaming and scurrying for safety. David glanced over toward the security booth, but no one was currently stationed there. His eyes went back to the glass doors to the outside. Where the hell were the police?

"You didn't really think it was over, did you?" the man asked.

"The police will be here any second," David warned. He was barely able to get the words out; his chest felt so tight. Staring at the gun, David thought of Benny and his last moments. Were they both going out at the hands of the same man?

"Not soon enough for you, I'm afraid."

David flinched when he heard the loud *thump* of a silenced gunshot. But he was shocked when he didn't feel anything right away. Had he been shot? In front of him, Appleton dropped his gun, fell to his knees. That's when David noticed blood spewing from a hole in the side of the man's head. What the hell? Then the white-haired man fell face forward onto the floor as blood pooled all around him. He heard more screams in the lobby, more shoes racing out building exits.

"You okay?" said a voice from David's left.

David jerked around, watched as a gray-haired man in his sixties wearing a sport coat quickly approached with a gun in his hand. Stepping up to David, the man put his gun away in a shoulder holster under his jacket.

"You hurt?" the man asked David, looking him up and down.

"I don't think so," David managed. "Are you with the police?"

"Hardly."

"Then who are you?"

"The guy who's going to help you make sure the right people get served justice."

"I don't understand."

"You will." The man pulled a tiny flash drive out of his jacket pocket. "Give this to the police when they get here."

David took the flash drive, confused. "Okay."

He suddenly heard sirens right around the corner of the building.

"Time for me to go," the man said. "Take care of yourself."

The man stepped around the dead body on the floor, then turned back to David.

"Hey, kid, I'm really sorry. I mean that."

David didn't know how to respond, so he didn't. He just watched as the man disappeared out a side exit. Seconds later, a host of police cars screeched to a stop in front of the building. Police officers jumped out of the vehicles and swiftly swarmed into the lobby with their guns drawn. David put his hands in the air out of reflex but was told by an approaching heavyset man in a brown jacket to put them down.

"You David?" he asked.

David nodded, feeling overwhelmed by the last few minutes.

"Detective Clark," the man introduced himself. "Who's this?"

The detective motioned toward the dead body on the floor.

"The man who killed my friend Benny, among others."

"You shot him?"

"No, sir."

"Then who did?"

"I honestly don't know, Detective."

"You okay?"

"Did you watch me with Marty Lyons?"

"Yeah, we got him. Good work."

"Where's Jen?" David asked.

"In the back of my Buick outside."

David rushed out of the building as more police cars arrived on the scene. When he found the Buick, Jen jumped out to meet him. She threw her arms around his neck before kissing him on the mouth. He pulled her in even closer, kissed her back.

"Are you okay?" Jen asked, holding his face in her hands.

"I am now."

"I should never have agreed to let you come here."

"I had to do it, Jen. I'm okay, I swear."

They both turned, watched the chaos for a moment. The glass of the building reflected the red and blue flashing lights. There must've been twelve police cars on-site. And David could hear even more sirens quickly approaching.

"Do you think it's over, David?" Jen asked.

"Yes, it's over."

He kissed her again.

Or just beginning, he thought. He had no idea where his life would go from here. But something inside told him he was going to be all right.

FORTY-TWO

Two months later

David stood on the sidewalk, stared up at the old three-story redbrick building.

He smiled, shook his head. It didn't quite have the glitz of the Frost Bank Tower, which sat directly across Congress Avenue behind him, but it would do just fine. Seconds later, the front door of the building opened, and Thomas Gray burst out onto the sidewalk toward him wearing blue jeans, a red polo, and penny loafers with no socks. He met David on the sidewalk with a huge smile, wrapped his arm around his shoulder.

"Welcome to Gray and Adams, Attorneys at Law," Thomas said enthusiastically.

"I thought you said we could go with Adams and Gray?"

"Ha! Details. You want to see your new office?"

"Sure. Lead the way."

They went inside the building and took the rickety stairwell up to the second level because the elevator was currently broken. Behind a wooden door in the front left corner, Thomas showed him into a greeting room surrounded by three tiny offices. All the rooms were smaller than Leo's paralegal office at Hunter & Kellerman. The whole office suite was less than half the size of H&K's lobby. There was no art on the walls, and there were no rugs on the floors. No receptionist. No assistants. No paralegals.

Thomas walked him into a front office with a window looking out over Congress. A cheap IKEA-like desk sat in the middle with an office chair behind it that looked like it had been purchased at Walmart. No more $3,000 Italian executive chairs. No more expansive views. David could hear music playing at Speakeasy next door and could smell alcohol fumes leaking through the cheap walls.

"What do you think, partner?" Thomas asked.

"It's perfect."

Thomas laughed. "Whatever, QB—we've got to start somewhere, right?"

"Seriously, Thomas, I'm happy to be here."

"Me, too." Thomas clapped him on the back. "I'll help you bring your boxes up later. I've got prospective foster parents coming here in a few minutes, so I need to get ready for that meeting. Lori has spaghetti in the mini-fridge in the back office, if you're hungry."

David stared out the window toward the Frost Bank Tower. It felt surreal that he'd survived a near-death encounter with Mark Appleton in the lobby just two months ago. Things had unfolded quickly in the aftermath: Marty Lyons had been arrested on the spot. The next day, the FBI had apprehended Joe Landon while he climbed into his private plane to flee the country. Both Lyons and Landon were currently in jail and awaiting trial. Because Appleton had tampered with the lobby security cameras just moments before he'd accosted David, the police had been unable to identify the mystery man who had inexplicably saved David's life before disappearing. But David had gotten word through Jen's detective friend that the contents of the flash drive included incriminating communications between Lyons and Landon.

Larue had immediately been released from jail. Even with a bum knee, the kid practically danced out the doors into freedom, where David and the boys from the Camp embraced him. David was doing everything he could to help the guys survive being back out on the streets after the Camp's tragic demise.

David opened his briefcase and pulled out a few notepads, some folders, and a box of pens. Reaching into the corner of the briefcase, he grabbed the small framed picture Jen had given him. It was the photo of him and Benny, arms draped over each other's shoulders. David smiled. Sure, the old man had used him as part of his intricate plan. But Benny had also opened his eyes to a different world. He was grateful for that.

Next, he pulled out the official paperwork for his recent purchase of twenty acres of undeveloped land out near the airport—Benny's land— which he'd been able to financially secure *before* giving official notice at Hunter & Kellerman. The purchase of the land was a start. He still had a lot of money to raise, but he was determined to somehow get there. Benny's dream of a village for the boys would become a reality one day soon.

David returned to the window, stared down at Congress. The image of him parking his old truck at the curb and walking inside the building across the street for the first time felt like a lifetime ago. Everything had changed. He was still a lawyer. He would just have different clients now. Most of them wore dirty clothes. Some even had missing teeth. And none of them could pay him much of anything. But he was okay with that.

His future had never felt so rich.

AUTHOR'S NOTE

Thirteen years ago, a man named Alan Graham, who founded an incredible nonprofit called Mobile Loaves & Fishes, walked me deep into the woods of East Austin late on a Tuesday night and forever changed my world. Never in my life had I been more warmly embraced by a group of caring men—men just like those at the Camp. As with David in *An Equal Justice*, this late-night experience changed *everything* for me. Since then, my wife and I have felt so privileged to serve our brothers and sisters on the streets.

I'm thrilled to tell you that Benny's fictional dream of creating a village for the boys has become a true-to-life reality here in Austin. We call it Community First! Village, a fifty-one-acre master-planned community that provides affordable, permanent housing and a supportive community for the disabled, chronically homeless. It has been the thrill of my life to have helped birth this dream into existence. You can find out more about my involvement with this incredible community on my website: www.chadzunker.com.

While I certainly hope *An Equal Justice* entertains you, I also hope it opens your mind and touches your heart. So the next time you may find yourself staring at the dirty face of someone begging for money on a sidewalk or holding a cardboard sign on a random street corner, you'll think about Benny's humanity—and you'll remember that a bigger story is being told. And maybe, just maybe, you're supposed to be part of that story.

ABOUT THE AUTHOR

Chad Zunker is the author of the bestselling Sam Callahan thriller series: *The Tracker*, *Shadow Shepherd*, and *Hunt the Lion*. He studied journalism at the University of Texas, where he was also on the football team. He has worked for some of the country's most powerful law firms and also has invented baby products that are sold all over the world. He lives in Austin with his wife, Katie, and their three daughters and is hard at work on the next David Adams legal thriller. For more information on the author and his writing, visit www.chadzunker.com.